Bello:
hidden talent rediscovered

Bello is a digital-only imprint of Pan Macmillan,
established to breathe new life into previously published,
classic books.

At Bello we believe in the timeless power of the imagination,
of a good story, narrative and entertainment, and we want to
use digital technology to ensure that many more readers
can enjoy these books into the future.

We publish in ebook and print-on-demand formats
to bring these wonderful books to new audiences.

www.panmacmillan.co.uk/bello

Margaret Dickinson

Born in Gainsborough, Lincolnshire, Margaret Dickinson moved to the coast at the age of seven and so began her love for the sea and the Lincolnshire landscape.

Her ambition to be a writer began early and she had her first novel published at the age of twenty-seven. This was followed by twenty-seven further titles including *Plough the Furrow*, *Sow the Seed* and *Reap the Harvest*, which make up her Lincolnshire Fleethaven trilogy.

Many of her novels are set in the heart of her home county, but in *Tangled Threads* and *Twisted Strands* the stories include not only Lincolnshire but also the framework knitting and lace industries of Nottingham.

Her 2012 and 2013 novels, *Jenny's War* and *The Clippie Girls*, were both top twenty bestsellers and her 2014 novel, *Fairfield Hall*, went to number nine on the *Sunday Times* bestseller list.

Margaret Dickinson

BRACKENBECK

First published in 1969 by Robert Hale

This edition published 2014 by Bello
an imprint of Pan Macmillan, a division of Macmillan Publishers Limited
Pan Macmillan, 20 New Wharf Road, London N1 9RR
Basingstoke and Oxford
Associated companies throughout the world

www.panmacmillan.co.uk/bello

ISBN 978-1-4472-9022-3 EPUB
ISBN 978-1-4472-9020-9 HB
ISBN 978-1-4472-9021-6 PB

Copyright © Margaret Dickinson, 1969

A CIP catalogue record for this book is available from the British Library.

Visit **www.panmacmillan.com** to read more about all our books
and to buy them. You will also find features, author interviews and
news of any author events, and you can sign up for e-newsletters
so that you're always first to hear about our new releases.

Author's Note

My writing career falls into two 'eras'. I had my first novel published at the age of twenty-five, and between 1968 and 1984 I had a total of nine novels published by Robert Hale Ltd. These were a mixture of light, historical romance, an action-suspense and one thriller, originally published under a pseudonym. Because of family commitments I then had a seven-year gap, but began writing again in the early nineties. Then occurred that little piece of luck that we all need at some time in our lives: I found a wonderful agent, Darley Anderson, and on his advice began to write saga fiction; stories with a strong woman as the main character and with a vivid and realistic background as the setting. Darley found me a happy home with Pan Macmillan, for whom I have now written twenty-one novels since 1994. Older, and with a maturity those seven 'fallow' years brought me, I recognize that I am now writing with greater depth and daring.

But I am by no means ashamed of those early works: they have been my early learning curve – and I am still learning! Originally, the first nine novels were published in hardback and subsequently in Large Print, but have never previously been issued in paperback or, of course, in ebook. So, I am thrilled that Macmillan, under their Bello imprint, has decided to reissue all nine titles.

Brackenbeck, published in 1969, was my second novel. At this time I was still working full- time as a clerk-typist and used to write in the evenings on a portable typewriter.

'O hard; when love and duty clash!'
– *The Princess* – Alfred Lord Tennyson

Chapter One

Doctor Katharine Harvey paused at the top of the hill overlooking the dale of Brackenbeck. Far below the small houses huddled together as if drawing comfort from each other's nearness. Somewhere nearby a rill tumbled down the hillside, twisting and widening into the swift flowing beck which encircled the houses and wound on through the dale.

Katharine shaded her eyes against the sun's glare and her gaze travelled upwards from the village, up the steep slopes of the far hills.

The quarry must be behind those hills, she thought.

As she picked up her black medical bag and heavy portmanteau and started down the hill, she felt she already knew Brackenbeck, even though this was her first visit. Anthony's letters were full of description of his beloved dale and amusing anecdotes about the people who lived there.

A small smile played at the corners of her gentle mouth. So like Anthony to forget to send a pony and trap to meet her at the station. In her ardent fight for equality between men and women, Katharine had to admit, though only to herself, that at this moment she would gladly have welcomed the usual comforts bestowed upon the weaker sex. Maybe Anthony could stride up and down his moorland, but to a city girl the roads were long and dusty.

Resolution hardened her smile – not one word of complaint would pass her lips during the following weeks. Her small feet trod the rough track purposefully and she tried not to think of the wear on the hem of her costume.

Neat in her plain brown skirt and matching jacket trimmed with velvet, Katharine hoped she looked worthy of the title 'doctor'. Her white blouse with its high neckline was demure enough, but she mistrusted the frivolity of her hat and wondered whether or not the villagers would do so too. It was a flat hat of brown straw, but trimmed with velvet and a white ostrich plume. It perched, rather coquettishly, on top of her shining auburn hair, which she wore in a simple, yet dignified, coil.

The narrow lane wound down into the village. Here and there Katharine saw patches of heather and clumps of bracken, but mostly the hillside where it was not hard, bare rock, was covered with rough grass.

Sheep grazed on the slopes and raised their heads to gaze sleepily at her as she passed. A small bird, with a curious spike of feathers at the back of its head, hovered above the grass, plunging and diving in idiotic acrobats. Katharine stopped to watch, but the bird soon fluttered away out of sight. The June day was fine and had been warm in London when she had left early that morning, but here a sharp breeze blew cold across the moors and Katharine shivered, knowing instinctively, the raw bleakness that winter on these moors would bring.

But I'll be back in London long before then, she promised herself.

To her left another track branched away from the main path. Apparently no one had used this track recently for the grass and bracken ran wild across it, covering in part the deep ruts worn by the waggons and carriages of long ago.

In the distance Katharine caught sight of grey walls and tall chimneys.

Curiosity claimed her and although she had walked three or four miles already she could not resist the temptation to follow the path. Leaving her heavy travelling bag in the grass at the side of the road, but keeping her medical bag, she pushed her way through the long grass. A pair of butterflies danced before her face and the pungent smell of sweet grass filled her nostrils. A stone wall with a wrought-iron gate surrounded a square, grey stone house. It was big, but not of gigantic proportions. It was a house belonging to a family with money, but not to the wealthy gentry.

Katharine peered through the gate. She could see the rough outline of the driveway curving up to the main entrance at the side of the house. The front windows faced out over the sloping garden overlooking the valley below. The house was obviously unoccupied. It looked deserted and lonely. Katharine felt the sadness of the place steal over her. The mullioned windows were sorrowful, misty with regret. It was a very old house, Katharine thought, at least two hundred years old, but still it stood, indestructible, on the hillside overlooking the dale.

The grounds, once beautiful she could imagine, were now overgrown and neglected. As she turned away, Katharine's eyes caught sight of a name-plate set in the stone wall, overgrown with green moss, which she scraped aside and read the ornate lettering 'Kendrick House'.

She frowned thoughtfully. Where had she heard that name before? Why, surely Anthony had spoken of someone of that name? She returned slowly to the road and with one backward glance at the desolate building, she picked up her bag again.

Katharine reached the village street and was surprised at its emptiness. Only a tabby cat sidled up and rubbed against her skirt, purring a welcome. No one else appeared from the closed doors, though she fancied she saw the movement of a curtain here and there. The only sound was the rattling wheels of a waggon some distance in front of her, making its way from the village up the track and over the hill in the direction of the quarry. And now, faintly, Katharine thought she could hear the echoing sounds from the quarry itself.

She turned a corner and left the village centre where the houses and cottages clustered either side of the narrow, cobbled street. Crossing the small stone bridge over the beck, she began to climb again to a house set apart and aloof from the villagers' dwellings. It was a well-proportioned house, surrounded on three sides by sycamore trees, whilst the view of the village from its front windows remained unimpaired. Without doubt, Katharine thought, it was the doctor's house. 'The Sycamores'. How unimaginative, she smiled to herself.

As she pushed open the gate, Katharine thought how different was this garden to that sad and neglected one at 'Kendrick House'. Here a smooth, sloping lawn was surrounded by well-ordered beds alive with multi-coloured blooms – tall delphiniums and lupins and heavy-headed peonies, red and pink, and roses just beginning to burst their buds.

The drive led up to four stone steps and on to a flagged stone terrace before another four steps brought her to the front door itself. Katharine lifted the heavy brass knocker in the cruel, yet fascinating, shape of a leopard's head.

She waited.

Moments later the door opened.

'Good afternoon,' Katharine said. 'You must be Mrs. Rigby?'

'Yes, miss,' was the curt reply.

'I am Dr. Harvey. Dr. Stafford expects me.'

'Yes, miss.'

And the woman opened the door for Katharine to enter.

Mrs. Rigby was a good deal taller than Katharine, though this could be well expected as Katharine's stature was small and slight, giving the mistaken impression of fragility.

The older woman's mode of dress was as severe as her countenance. Her blouse was high-necked with long, close-fitting sleeves. The skirt, black like her blouse, fell in severe lines to the floor, flaring slightly from some eighteen inches above the hem.

The hallway, Katharine saw as she stepped into it, was dark and austere. All the woodwork was dark oak and the wallpaper was a dingy floral design. Obviously Anthony could not be bothered with domestic interests and Mrs. Rigby looked the type who resented change of any kind.

'Dr. Stafford is in the drawing-room, miss. This way, if you please.'

The woman led the way, her head high, her hands clasped in front of her at waist height. Katharine felt Mrs. Rigby's hostility not only in her greeting but in the rigid set of the shoulders and unyielding straightness of back.

Mrs. Rigby opened the door on to a large room and stood aside for Katharine to enter.

At the far end of the room Dr. Anthony Stafford sat in a deep leather armchair, his foot and ankle, heavily encased in white bandage, resting on a footstool.

'Katharine, my dear girl,' he smiled, slapping the arm of his chair. 'Thank God you've come to save me from this boredom.'

'Hello Anthony,' Katharine laughed, never failing to be cheered by his boisterous good humour. 'How's the ankle?'

'Deuced painful. It's good of you to come at such short notice.'

Katharine's face sobered swiftly. She glanced back at Mrs. Rigby, unwilling to confide in Anthony in his housekeeper's presence.

'That will be all, Mrs. Rigby,' Anthony said.

'Thank you, sir.' Her glance rested again on Katharine. Mrs. Rigby sniffed in contempt and left the room.

'Dear me,' remarked Anthony, 'you don't seem to have enslaved Mrs. Rigby as yet.'

Katharine smiled ruefully.

'No. As I was going to say, there are very few places where a lady-doctor is welcome. I'm glad you did call on me, Anthony. I'm still without employment.'

Anthony moved uneasily in his chair.

'Sit down, lass, sit down.'

Katharine noticed the immediate change in his tone.

'Kate – I'll have to be honest with you.' Anthony's blue eyes looked into hers with compassion. 'Apart from me, you're not going to be very welcome here.'

Katharine nodded.

'I guessed as much. So why did you send for me?'

Anthony leaned over and knocked out his pipe on the grey stone fireplace.

'Several reasons, I suppose. One – I thought you were in need of occupation whilst you're waiting to hear about your appointment to the children's ward at St. Bernadette's Hospital. You haven't heard, I suppose?' He looked up eagerly.

Katharine shook her head.

'Secondly,' Anthony continued, 'I thought the "challenge" might be good for you and, believe me, there's going to be one. And lastly – but by no means least of all,' and his blue eyes regarded her intently as he added softly, 'I wanted to see you again, Kate.'

'And you wanted a good dose of feminine sympathy,' Katharine teased him. 'I doubt you get it from Mrs. Rigby.'

And their laughter filled the room.

But Katharine was to find that in the next few weeks laughter did not come easily.

That first evening passed pleasantly enough in Anthony's company, but all the while the thought of tomorrow's surgery hung like a dark cloud at the back of her mind.

At seven o'clock the kitchen maid served their dinner, under Mrs. Rigby's supervision.

'Have you any more servants, Anthony?' Katharine asked, when Mrs. Rigby and the young girl had left the room.

'No, just Mrs. Rigby and Jane.'

'One "upper" and one "lower" servant,' Katharine smiled. 'Is Mrs. Rigby married or rather, has she been, or is it one of these courtesy titles given to a housekeeper?'

'No, she was married. Lost her husband in a quarry accident about twenty years ago. She has no family. She came with the practice, you might say,' he added smiling.

'You mean she was here with Dr. Leverton?'

'Yes, *and* she doesn't let me forget it.'

'My father could only afford to employ one overworked servant girl,' Katharine said, 'I used to feel sorry for her – up at dawn and hardly ever finished her work before nine or ten at night.'

'Yes, it must be a hard life for some of these young girls with no education to speak of and yet obliged to earn their living. I don't think it's *too* hard here. I have a man in the village come each day to do the heavy work – chopping wood and so forth. And he does the garden. Mrs. Rigby takes charge of all the cooking, of course, and takes my messages, plus, I believe, a little light dusting if she feels so disposed,' he grinned. 'And Jane does the rest.'

Katharine eyed him over her soup spoon.

'Mmmm,' she said with meaning.

'Let's change the subject,' Anthony teased her, 'or I can see by the glint in your eye that I shall be getting a full-scale lecture on women's rights.'

After they had dined and had lingered by the fire, reminiscing about their university life and exchanging confidences until quite late, Mrs. Rigby once again appeared at the drawing-room door.

'Miss Harvey stopping here, is she, sir?'

Anthony looked at his housekeeper out of the corner of his eye.

'You prepared her room as I requested, didn't you?'

'Yes, sir. But I thought – well –' Mrs. Rigby sniffed and altered her line of conversation. 'Shall I show her the room, sir?'

'Thank you, no. I can direct Dr. Harvey adequately, I believe.'

The thin lips were pursed tightly and the eyes glittered with disapproval.

'Goodnight then, sir – miss.'

The door closed with a sharp click of annoyance.

'Take no notice of her, Kate.'

'But what did she mean? Why the question about my staying here?'

Anthony laughed.

'You're alone in this house with me, Katharine Harvey – for the night, except for Mrs. Rigby and Jane, neither of whom, being servants, can suffice as a chaperon. Can't you imagine what the village folk think to that? Mrs. Rigby did her utmost to persuade me to book a room for you at the "Delvers' Haven" in the village.'

Katharine stared at him – wide-eyed.

'Oh Anthony – I never thought. How foolish of me. I thought there was someone else in the house too. I mean, I thought –' she rushed on hastily, 'that Mrs. Rigby's presence would be sufficient. I confess I've never before found myself in such circumstances.'

'We're a strange folk here,' Anthony said. 'Some of their ideas of propriety are early Victorian – others so liberal-minded as to shock even you, Kate. It's knowing what they expect of you – there's the difficulty. But you don't mind, Kate, do you?'

7

'*I* don't – no. But what is everyone going to think – to say? It'll make things awkward for you, as well as for me, and you've got to stay here.'

'My dear Kate, it won't worry me – you should know that.'

And Katharine did know it. Whatever did worry the good-humoured Anthony? His genial bantering had kept her in good spirits the whole evening.

'You should know how progressively minded I am or I would not have befriended one of these dreadful suffragettes,' he said, the mischievous twinkle in his eyes belying his sober tones.

'We're not "dreadful",' Katharine retorted defensively.

'I know, I know, I'm only teasing. Did I not use to help you, Kate? Have you forgotten?'

'No, no, of course not, Anthony. But, for a moment, I just thought that now you're back amongst your own people, perhaps . . .'

'That perhaps I'd gone back to their narrow-minded way of life?'

She nodded.

'I'm wrong, I see,' she said. 'And besides, I no longer take an active part in suffragism. I can't risk getting involved, maybe arrested even, now I bear the title "doctor".'

'No, but on the other hand, you're helping their cause all the more by meeting that very challenge of becoming a doctor,' Anthony said.

He shook his head slowly and sighed.

'It'll be hard, very hard, to overcome all the opposition you're going to meet.'

'I know,' she said simply, 'and it'll start right here at tomorrow morning's surgery.'

'I fear it will,' was Anthony's only reply – the only possible reply.

Katharine found her bedroom was depressingly cold and sparsely furnished. She had known worse, but the whole house needed the cheerful touch of a woman's work – with love and care behind it, not just as an onerous duty as no doubt Mrs. Rigby looked upon her work.

Everything was clean and neat but dull and uninteresting. Like the rest of the house the woodwork was brown. The bed, with an iron bedstead, had a lumpy mattress covered with sheets, two thin blankets and a patchwork quilt.

The small window overlooked the back of the house and in the darkness Katharine could see the black shapes of the trees growing close to the house and hear the wind moaning softly in the branches.

Katharine undressed quickly and slid, shivering, beneath the sheets. She watched the moon, at first hidden by scudding clouds, then brilliant, silhouetting the branches of the trees outside her window as they swayed in the wind.

She had thought she would find sleep impossible, but to her surprise she slept heavily after her long journey northwards from London.

The following morning Katharine was awakened by Jane tapping on the door bringing with her all the necessary equipment for her to take a morning bath.

'Mrs. Rigby said you'd be sure to want a bath ev'ry morning, miss.'

And without waiting for a reply the girl spread a huge bathmat on the floor and heaved a hip-bath on to it. The bath was varnished on the outside to a mud-colour and the inside was cream enamel, badly chipped, Katharine noticed. The girl arranged around the bath a large towel and smaller face towel, the soap dish, sponge bowl and large jug of cold water, all matching earthenware decorated with huge blue cornflowers on a white background.

She disappeared, re-appearing some minutes later with a huge can of near-boiling water.

''Tis ready, miss,' Jane said and disappeared again.

Katharine bathed quickly, having poured in too much cold water to enjoy it.

As she dressed, shivering, Katharine thought ruefully that in enlightened circles the bedroom fire was supposed to be lit before a lady took her morning bath. Here, no doubt, it was felt to be unnecessary, for the women in this dale would be healthy, hardy creatures, not expecting, nor receiving, any such indulgence.

Later, having breakfasted with Anthony and received his

instructions, Katharine found her way to the west side of the house which was reserved for the doctor's surgery. A side entrance between the waiting room and the doctor's room afforded complete isolation from the doctor's private residence.

Katharine familiarised herself with Anthony's instruments before the opening of the surgery and was amused, but delighted, to find that he possessed a quantity of modern equipment. She smiled. Certainly the frugality practised in Anthony's domestic affairs was not repeated in his surgery.

At nine o'clock exactly, Katharine rang the bell to summon the first patient and waited. And she waited.

No doubt the patients had not yet arrived.

She walked about the room, reading the books in Anthony's bookcase, touching the bottles in the cabinet and finally coming to stand before the mirror over the fireplace. She looked at herself and noticed that her eyes were wide and her cheeks a little paler than their usual healthy olive colour. Her auburn hair was smoothed back from her face into a coil at the nape of her neck. Restlessly, she turned away and sat down at the desk again. She picked up a pen and twisted it through her fingers, her eyes on the door, her ears straining for the sounds of the arrival of a patient.

Suddenly, the loneliness engulfed her. She felt almost foolish sitting there wishing for some sick person to come through the door in need of her care and attention, wanting her.

'This is foolish nonsense,' she told herself springing up and going to the door. Making sure that there was no one in the waiting-room, she left the surgery and went through the house to the drawing-room.

Anthony was seated again in his armchair, reading the morning paper.

'Your patients seem in remarkably good health, Dr. Stafford. Not one seems to require my attention.'

Anthony looked at her quizzically over the top of his newspaper. He raised his shaggy eyebrows philosophically.

'It's sometimes like that. Most of them are too busy to be ill round here.'

'Rubbish,' Katharine said sharply, pacing the floor, 'and you know it. You're trying to console me.'

'My dear Kate, give them time. It's only half past nine. You've another half an hour before surgery's officially over – and then they'll still roll up.'

'Well if they don't come, I can't very well go out into the streets looking for patients, can I?'

'Precisely, Kate,' Anthony grinned.

'Oh, you're impossible,' Katharine said, but she had to laugh.

Back in the surgery she found a wizened old man in the waiting-room.

'Would you come this way, please,' she bade him.

He looked at her strangely but followed her. He stood uncertainly in the doorway of the doctor's room whilst Katharine seated herself at the desk.

'Please sit down.'

The old man's shrewd eyes darted about the room coming to rest on her with a belligerent glare.

'Where's t'doctor?'

'I'm a doctor.'

'I want Dr. Stafford.'

'Doctor Stafford has sprained his ankle badly and cannot walk. I am taking over his practice for a short while.'

'I want nowt to do wi' wimmin doctors,' the old man wheezed, and coughed painfully.

'You seem to have a nasty cough there,' Katharine said ignoring his remark. 'Let's see if we can give you something to ease it.'

She rose and went towards the medicine cabinet.

'Ah don't want none o' tha potions, miss, thank 'ee. More an' like it'll be poison.'

Katharine whirled to face him, a sharp retort on her lips. But instead she sighed. There was no point in losing her temper. Better to keep her dignity.

'Good day to thee,' the old man turned away. 'I'll be waiting till t'doctor is better 'imself.'

The old man's visit caused Katharine more despondency than ever and even Anthony's teasing could not lift her from depression.

At last even his levity faded and he told her seriously,

'Katharine, you're going to meet a great deal of opposition in this world because you're a pioneer almost as a woman entering the field of medicine. I know you had a valiant battle at university and you won. You qualified. But the fight's not over.'

'I know,' she sighed. 'If it hadn't been for your support then, I might never have finished the course.'

'It was lucky for me too that I met you. I don't know what I'd have done in those early days without your friendship. The city was just as strange to me as the country is to you.'

'I've always imagined that country folk were more friendly than townsfolk,' Katharine said.

'Don't you believe it. They live in the past. Why, no one here in Brackenbeck owns a horseless carriage though they do say that Jim Kendrick is sorely tempted.'

'That's the name – I thought I'd heard it before. You used to talk about him at university – I remember now. I saw an empty house called "Kendrick House" on my way down into the village. Is it his house?'

There was a pause whilst Anthony filled his pipe and moved his leg to a more comfortable position on the stool.

'Ah, I was coming to him.'

The silence deepened as Anthony lit his pipe, the blue smoke curling upwards as he drew and puffed.

'Jim Kendrick is enemy number one as far as you're concerned.'

'But you said, I remember, when you spoke of him years ago, that the whole valley idolised him.'

'Ah, they do. That's just it, Kate. Young and old, men, women and children – all are Jim Kendrick's willing slaves. And so, what he says goes.'

'Then how does it affect me?'

'Because he will not welcome you, and so – nor will anyone else.'

'Why ever not? He doesn't even know me.'

'Kate, Jim doesn't like women. And he likes women doctors even less.'

'Why?'

'It's a long story and if I tell you, it's in strict confidence – he's not a man to like his private affairs noised abroad.'

'Of course, Anthony.'

'Jim Kendrick lives in the centre of the village in a little cottage of his own. His sister, Mary, and her husband, Tom Gifford, live next door. They have a small son, by the way, of two. Jim's father lives in the next dale now. They hardly ever see him. He's a cussed old devil, rich as a king and mean as they come. He, the father, still owns "Kendrick House", but doesn't want to live there, and doesn't want anyone else to live there either. So his son and daughter live in cottages in the village.'

'But I thought Jim Kendrick owned Brackenbeck quarry?'

'So he does. He worked like a slave, still does for that matter, and eight years ago when he was only twenty-five, mind you, the chap who owned the quarry, Simon Johnson, drank himself to death and Jim was able to buy the quarry with his savings. If anyone deserved to get on, it's Jim, for there's few that work as hard.'

'You were close friends with him, weren't you, Anthony?'

'Ay.' Anthony drew on his pipe and leant back in the chair, his head resting on the leather back, his eyes roaming the ceiling but seeing the days of his boyhood.

'There were good times and bad. Good mainly for me and bad for Jim.' He had a very unhappy boyhood,' Anthony continued. 'His mother and father fought like cat and dog and finally his mother, having money of her own, walked out on them. Jim was only fourteen and Mary a wee lass of six. Jim never forgave his mother, you understand, and apart from his sister, he'll have nothing to do with women.'

'I see,' Katharine said slowly. 'He must be rather narrow-minded, though, to consider all women in the same category as his mother.'

Anthony shrugged.

'He just built a wall round himself, Kate. Even I, who consider myself his best friend to this day, can't talk about his family to him. But,' Anthony waved his pipe at her, 'mark my words, if that man ever falls in love, he'll fall harder than anyone I know and woe betide the woman who crosses him.'

Katharine shuddered.

'He sounds fearsome on his own without being backed by everyone in the village. Still, I'm not one to run away from a fight, Anthony Stafford, seeing as you've put me in the middle of one.'

Anthony grinned.

'That's my Kate.'

Katharine spent the day in and around Anthony's house. She did not like to venture far for fear someone needed her medical attention and she was missing.

The next morning she found the surgery empty again and not even a disgruntled old man put in an appearance.

The day was fine and warm and during the afternoon Anthony, tired of sitting indoors, decided he could hobble out into the garden.

'I'll need your help, Kate,' his eyes twinkled merrily, and he put his arm about her slim shoulders and, pretending to lean heavily on her, they went out into the front garden giggling at Anthony's hopping gait just like two school children.

Coming up the drive was Mrs. Rigby, who observed their hilarity with reprobation. Katharine watched the expression of disdain upon the woman's face as she neared them. 'Good afternoon, Mrs. Rigby,' Anthony called as he settled himself comfortably on the garden seat. 'That was a fine lunch you gave us.'

The woman mellowed a little beneath Anthony's charm, but her glance at Katharine held no trace of friendship.

'Mr. Kendrick's on 'is way to see you, sir.'

'Good,' bellowed Anthony. 'Make us some tea, Mrs. Rigby, there's a lamb.'

Mrs. Rigby actually smiled. It was plain to see that if there was a soft spot under her flint-like countenance, it was for Dr. Stafford.

Anthony and Katharine waited in the garden for the arrival of Jim Kendrick. Katharine felt uncommonly nervous, as if her fate rested with this stranger. Certainly she knew her reception in

Brackenbeck depended upon his attitude towards her, for the villagers would follow his lead. But why should she feel that this man, whom she had yet to meet, could alter the whole course of her life?

Chapter Two

Katharine saw Jim Kendrick long before he reached Anthony's gate. He walked up the slope with easy strides. He was a giant of a man, broad-shouldered and lithe. His black hair glinted in the sunlight. As he neared them, she could see his eyes were hidden almost beneath heavy black eyebrows drawn together in a perpetual frown. His face was tanned and his arms, tanned also to a deep bronze, were muscular. He was dressed in workman's clothes and heavy boots, and she guessed he had come straight from the quarry. But despite the appearance of his clothes, there was a proud air about the way he walked as if he were answerable to no man – or woman.

'Hello there, Anthony,' he greeted, his voice a rich bass as one might expect.

'Hello, Jim. I'd like you to meet a friend of mine, Dr. Harvey. She's kindly come to stand in for me whilst I'm laid up with this ankle.'

The frown deepened and now, as he stood before her, she looked up into his dark eyes and tried to smile. She found no answering smile of welcome, but he did, after a moment's hesitation, take the hand she held out to him. His grasp was firm and warm, yet the words he spoke belied his touch.

'I'm afraid I cannot welcome you to our village, Miss Harvey. My men would not welcome a woman doctor.'

His voice held traces of his Yorkshire heritage, but, like Anthony, his dialect was less noticeable than with most of the people of Brackenbeck.

'I'm sorry you feel that way, Mr. Kendrick,' Katharine said quietly and with dignity. 'But perhaps you and your men will change your minds if your families are sick and in need of help whilst Dr. Stafford is indisposed.'

Jim Kendrick jerked his head.

'There's a doctor in the next valley could attend to us fine. Anthony had no need to bring you here.'

'A doctor has his patients' welfare at heart, Mr. Kendrick. Dr. Stafford acted in the interest of his patients in bringing a qualified doctor to be resident in this valley.'

'Come, come,' Anthony laughed. 'You've only just met and yet here you both are with your hackles up.'

Katharine smiled, but Jim remained silent, his brown gaze seeming to take in Katharine's appearance.

She felt he was appraising her strength and ability, and finding her lacking in both.

Automatically her head went higher and she met his gaze unflinchingly.

At last Jim turned away and spoke in unhurried tones to Anthony.

'I came to see if there was aught I could do – to help make arrangements about another doctor, but it seems you've taken matters into your own hands.'

'Jim,' Anthony said, 'give the lass a chance. She's a qualified doctor.'

'Why hasn't she a practice of her own then?'

Anthony glanced at Katharine.

'Because I am waiting to hear if my application to join the children's ward at a London hospital has been accepted,' Katharine told him.

'I see.' He turned back to Anthony. 'Look, it's only that I'm concerned about her being able to cope if there were an accident. Some of these things are no sight for a woman. What if she faints?'

Anthony's loud laughter filled the air.

'Katharine – faint?' He slapped his thigh. 'You underestimate her, old man. She's as tough as they come.'

Jim shook his head slowly.

'I must be old-fashioned, Miss Harvey. Maybe I am. I'm sorry, but I cannot accept that you can do the work of a man. Good-day to you both.'

And he left them as swiftly as he had come.

All her fears had been justified. This man disturbed Katharine more than she cared to admit. She thought she had become used to the prejudice she was bound to meet in her chosen profession, new to it as women were, but Jim Kendrick's refusal to accept her hurt far more than she had thought possible.

'Don't let him worry you, lass. Though I'm more sorry than I can say that he's acting this way, I expected as much,' Anthony said, for once his handsome face sober.

'Don't let it bother you, Anthony, after all I shan't be here for long,' Katharine answered and was startled to see the pain cross Anthony's face.

'Is your ankle hurting, Anthony?'

'No,' he said grimly. 'Forget it.'

But his swift change of attitude to one so contrary to his nature puzzled Katharine.

Mrs. Rigby's hostility did little to ease Katharine's feelings for the villagers and it wasn't until she had been in the valley for over a week that she received her first patient at morning surgery.

A fresh-faced young woman entered the consulting-room carrying a little boy of about two years old in her arms. The child was big for his age and a handsome little fellow, Katharine saw, but obviously running a fever.

'Is Dr. Stafford not here?' The woman paused uncertainly in the doorway.

'No, but I am a doctor. Can I help?'

'Well, I don't rightly know . . .'

'Please come and sit down.'

The woman came in and set the child down to stand on the floor. The little boy whimpered and swayed slightly clutching at his mother's skirts.

'It's little Tommy,' the woman explained. 'He seems reet poorly. Got a cough and he's lost his voice.'

Katharine knelt before the child.

'Come here, Tommy, and let's have a look at you,' she said gently.

The child eyed her mistrustfully, his eyes swollen and red, his face hot.

Swiftly and gently Katharine examined him.

'He's got laryngitis – not severely though. You must take him home immediately and keep him in bed. I'll call this afternoon.'

Katharine rose and crossed over to the medicine cabinet.

'Here give him a teaspoonful of this in water every three hours. And mind you keep him warm and don't let him try to talk much if you can help it. Give him warm drinks of milk, too. Now can I have your name and tell me where you live, please?'

'Well, I'm Mrs. Gifford. But I don't think you ought to call at t'house, miss. Tom, that's my husband, wouldn't like you to come. He's at work and doesn't know I've come here, d'you see?'

'But Mrs. Gifford, your child needs my care. I must call.'

'Oh dear.' The woman blushed with anxiety, torn between fear of her husband and worry for her sick child.

Katharine felt a rush of pity for her. She could see that the woman herself had no qualms about accepting Katharine as a doctor. It was only her husband's antagonism which caused her dilemma.

'Will you call this afternoon about three o'clock, then, miss. He'll be back at work then. He needn't know.'

'All right, Mrs. Gifford, for the sake of your child, I will.'

'Thank you, oh thank you.'

The woman's gratitude was touching, but it made Katharine angry to think that Mrs. Gifford went in such fear of her husband.

'Tom idolises his brother-in-law, Kate,' Anthony told her when she related her morning experience to him. 'The only way you'll win over the folk of Brackenbeck is to have Jim Kendrick on your side.'

'And I've about as much chance of doing that as flying,' Katharine retorted.

The afternoon was again devoid of callers and Katharine chafed against her uselessness until it was time to go into the village and see Tommy Gifford.

Had it not been for the disquiet in her mind she would have greatly enjoyed the walk from Anthony's house down the hill to the Giffords' cottage. The sun was warm and the beck bright and bubbling. In the village street several children were engrossed in a game of hop-scotch, some almost too small to play were bullied by the bigger ones. Katharine paused to watch, smiling as she recalled playing the very same game herself years ago.

She sighed and moved on. How quickly time passed, she thought. It seemed no time since she had been the same age as these children living with her parents in London. Her father had been a general practitioner in a poorer part of the city. They'd never had much money for his patients were rarely able to pay their bills. But Dr. Harvey was fortunate in that his wife, and later his daughter, Katharine, shared his devotion to medicine and to the patients. Now, both her parents were dead, but not before they had seen her accepted into medical school and known that she was carrying on the family work.

An only child, Katharine was often lonely and had it not been for her strength of character and resolve she might well have suffered greatly from the lack of the affection of a family.

She walked along the cobbled street, smiling at the women who sat in the doorways of their cottages, or passed her on the street. A few smiled hesitantly, several avoided her gaze and looked towards the ground, but the majority, much to Katharine's dismay, returned her greeting with a stony expression of disapproval.

Katharine reached the two cottages belonging to Jim Kendrick, where he lived with the Giffords next door.

She knocked firmly at the green door and waited.

After a few minutes it opened and the scared face of Mary Gifford peered round it.

'Oh, come in, Miss Harvey, quickly.'

Katharine entered and stood in the front parlour into which the front door opened. The room was small and overcrowded with furniture. A large table occupied the centre of the room surrounded by the four chairs. A dresser, overflowing with china ornaments and what was obviously the 'best' tea service, stood against one wall. From the rag mat in front of the range, a cat eyed Katharine sleepily.

'I don't want it to get about the village, d'you see, and get back to my Tom,' Mary Gifford was saying.

'Mrs. Gifford, your child is ill. Surely your husband cannot object to my attending him?'

'I don't think he'd like it. You see, Jim says . . .'

'Say no more, I quite understand. Now, if I can see the little chap, the sooner I can leave.'

'This way, then, miss.'

Katharine climbed the narrow stairway to an attic-like bedroom where the small boy lay in bed. He seemed a little better than at the surgery, no doubt the warm bed helped, but Katharine saw he was still ill enough to be kept in bed and would be so for some days.

She tried to impress upon Mrs. Gifford the need for her to visit Tommy again, but the young woman's fear of her husband and brother gave her strength in another direction – to resist Katharine's pleading.

Whilst they were still arguing, downstairs again out of the child's hearing, they heard footsteps on the path and the sound of men's voices.

'Oh no, 'tis Tom and Jim, home early. Oh, my goodness . . .'

Escape was impossible. Katharine had no fear of either of them, but she felt desperately sorry for the nervous woman, who wrung her hands and bit her lip, as the front door opened.

Tom Gifford entered first and stood aside as Jim bent his head and stepped into the room. Immediately his huge frame seemed to fill the tiny room and his presence overawed the company.

'Good afternoon, Miss Harvey,' he said politely. 'I see you have met my sister. This is her husband, Mr. Gifford.'

Katharine presumed he had no idea of the reason for her visit, thinking, no doubt, that her call was social, to which he could have no objections.

'Tom,' Mary began as Katharine and he were shaking hands.

'It's young Tommy. He weren't well this morning, so I took him to the doctor and . . .'

Katharine saw the frown on Jim Kendrick's face deepen and Tom Gifford glanced from his wife's anxious face to Katharine's and at last, to Jim's face.

'What's to do?'

'Your son has laryngitis, Mr. Gifford, but with careful treatment he'll be up and about in a few days.'

'Nay, 'tis nowt but croup. Ah've seen it afore,' Tom Gifford laughed. 'Don't mamby-pamby the lad, woman.'

'The child is ill, Mr. Gifford, and must be kept in bed.'

Tom laughed again, whilst Katharine felt her temper rise.

Tom Gifford opened the door.

'I'll bid you good-day, Miss Harvey, we have no need of your services here.'

'You're being extremely foolish in refusing my care for your son.'

She turned to Jim, her green eyes flashing.

'I'm not unaware that the fault lies with you, Mr. Kendrick. It seems the whole village obeys your command. Let me tell you something, if anything happens to your nephew, or to anyone else in this village whilst I am here, it will be *your* fault, not mine.'

And with that she marched out of the cottage.

Not until she reached the bridge did she stop to think. Sighing heavily, she sat down on the low wall of the packhorse bridge and gazed at the rushing water of the beck.

She did not regret her harsh words, even though perhaps they were hasty, for they were fully justified.

Jim Kendrick, she thought, was an arrogant, conceited man, who ill-used the villagers' respect for him.

'I never want to see him again,' she said aloud, but knew in that instant that if she were never to see him again she would know a sense of loss.

She laughed wryly.

'I just like someone to fight with, that's all,' she told herself.

Katharine saw a child running towards her along the beck side. A small thin little girl in a worn cotton dress.

Katharine looked down again at the water and thought the child had passed by, so that she was surprised when the steps slowed and stopped beside her. She felt the child's hand grasp her arm and she turned swiftly to meet the upturned gaze of wide brown eyes. The thin, pale face was smudged with dirt and showed signs of recent tears.

'Are t'doctor?'

'Yes.'

The small fingers tightened on Katharine's wrist and pulled at her with urgency.

'Coom, see Grannie Banroyd. She's reet bad.'

Katharine hurried after the child, who ran ahead of her along the cobbled street, from time to time stopping to look back at her, urging her to hurry, then running ahead as if she could not bear to delay.

They reached a tiny cottage on the outskirts of the village.

The child disappeared through the low door and Katharine followed. The interior of the hovel, for it was little more than that, was dark and smelt musty. The furniture, old and decrepit, was covered with a film of dust. Pots and pans cluttered the hearth. The table held the remains of an unappetising meal – watery broth and thick, grey bread.

The child had run to the far corner of the room, where, Katharine saw as her eyes became accustomed to the shadows, a frail old woman lay on a bedstead. A thin blanket covered her and she clutched an old, crocheted shawl about her rounded shoulders. Her face was wrinkled and wizened, and white, wispy hair framed her face in untidy tufts. Her eyes were closed and every few seconds a soft moan escaped her parted lips.

'Grannie,' the child whispered. ''Tis doctor.'

The eyelids fluttered open and slowly the old woman turned her head to look at Katharine. The moaning grew louder and she shook her head painfully.

The child recoiled – wide-eyed and fearful.

'Doctor – I want t'doctor.'

The child, thinking the old woman misunderstood, leaned forward again and repeated her words.

'Grannie. *'Tis doctor!*'

Her grandmother lifted herself feebly and waved her bony hand.

'No – no – not 'er. Dr. Stafford.'

And she fell back against the pillow as a spasm of coughing seized her.

The child shrank back in fear and disappointment. Katharine touched the small girl kindly on the shoulder but the child shook off her hand and turned her back.

Katharine watched helplessly as the child's thin shoulders shook with her sobbing. The old woman's coughing quietened. Katharine turned to her.

'Mrs. Banroyd. Let me help you, please. Dr. Stafford has sprained his ankle. I *am* a qualified doctor . . .'

Katharine felt the familiar resentment rising within her, but kept her voice calm. After all, the old woman was very ill with bronchitis, as far as Katharine could see without a proper examination, and the sick cannot think rationally, she reminded herself.

The small face on the grey pillow turned determinedly from side to side in negation.

'If you won't let me examine you, at least let me bring you some medicine for your cough?'

Again no response.

She could not forcibly examine Grannie Banroyd, Katharine knew, neither could she get her to take any treatment, but at least she could bring a bottle of medicine to the cottage in the hope that the old woman would weaken in her resolve as her coughing became worse, and take some of the mixture.

Katharine left the cottage a little while later without either the child or her grandmother having spoken to her again. A cool breeze whipped down the narrow street as she walked back through the village.

Katharine felt helpless against the stubbornness of these people and was ashamed of her powerlessness.

Reaching the house and surgery she quickly prepared the medicine and was about to return immediately to the Banroyds' cottage, determined not to be beaten by the stubborn old woman and resolving this time to examine her, when Mrs. Rigby knocked and entered the room.

'Dr. Stafford would like a word with you, miss. He saw you return. He's in the drawing-room.' And without waiting for a reply, the housekeeper left the room.

'What is it, Anthony?' Katharine asked as she entered the drawing-room.

'Ah, there you are, Katharine.'

She noticed at once the frown on his face. An expression so unusual on Anthony's cheerful countenance that immediately she felt a sense of panic. Something must be seriously amiss for Anthony to be disgruntled.

'Mrs. Rigby tells me that Grannie Banroyd has bronchitis again. Shall you go down at once and see her?'

'I've already been. In fact, I'm on my way back there now with this.'

She held the bottle out for him to see. He took it, opened it and smelt it.

Then he nodded.

'That's all right. It's what I normally give her.'

'I'm glad you approve, doctor,' Katharine said sharply.

'Now, now, Kate,' Anthony said, trying to pacify her. 'Surely I've a right to maintain an interest in my patients even if I am laid up?'

'I'm sorry, Anthony,' Katharine said immediately. 'But Grannie Banroyd would not let me examine her and her refusal has distressed me.'

Anthony shrugged and grunted.

'No more than I would expect. Tell you what. Take that back and say I've made it up.'

Katharine was about to retort that she had no intention of succumbing to the old woman's whims, but the words died on her lips as she realised suddenly that if subterfuge was the only way to get Mrs. Banroyd to take treatment then that was the way it must be. The patient came before her own personal pride.

She sighed.

'Very well, Anthony. By the way, I was going to try whatever diaphoretic remedies I could, a mustard and linseed-meal poultice, for a start, then perhaps a simple linseed poultice – do you agree?'

'Of course, though it may be a little late for that if the attack is somewhat advanced – however, it may help. But I doubt she'll let you, and you can hardly enforce such treatment. But do your best, Kate.'

'I think one or two applications at least would be of value,' she replied.

When she returned to the cottage the child was still sitting exactly as Katharine had left her, crying quietly. Turning to Grannie Banroyd, she found that the old lady was now too weak to resist her and Katharine was able to examine her.

But her examination was futile. She had been called too late. She applied poultices to the woman's shrunken body and finally stayed until late in the evening, returning early the next morning and remaining all day at the cottage doing whatever she could – preparing steam inhalers and administering drugs herself in a desperate effort to save the old woman's life, which was surely slipping away. But she was fighting a losing battle against all odds. It was impossible to achieve satisfactory conditions in this hovel for her patient, apart from the fact that the disease had been so far advanced when she had been called.

It was too late, and Katharine knew she could not save the frail old lady.

That evening, quite late, as she was leaving the Banroyds' cottage and making her way back to Anthony's, Katharine was confronted by the one person whom she particularly did not wish to encounter at that time.

She was weary. Her back ached. Her medical bag was a heavy lump of rock in her hand. And her spirits had sunk to their lowest ebb ever. She had to pass Jim Kendrick's small cottage and as she did so, Katharine saw the door open and the lamp light flood the cobbled street.

'Miss Harvey.'

His deep voice rang out into the night. She stopped and turned to face him. The light was on her face, but his in the shadow, so that she felt the disadvantage of not being able to read the expression on his face.

But could she not guess it from his voice? His tone was cold and his words unfriendly.

'Good evening, Miss Harvey. You're abroad late, are you not?'

'I've been with Mrs. Banroyd all day.' Katharine knew her voice to be toneless with fatigue.

'How is she?'

Slowly Katharine shook her head.

'I'm afraid it's only a matter of a day or two.'

'What? You mean she is going to die?'

'I'm very much afraid so. If only . . .'

'Yes, Miss Harvey. If only . . .' And although the words were unspoken between them, she knew he was implying 'if only Dr. Stafford had been available instead of an ineffectual woman.'

Katharine raised her head defiantly.

'I was going to say, if only she had called me days ago, then, perhaps, more could have been done.'

'I'm sure you have done your best.'

Katharine could not fail to recognise the irony in his words and she knew also that he had meant her to do so.

'And you mean my best is not good enough?'

'She's going to die, you say,' Jim said quietly.

Katharine's shoulders drooped. She nodded, not trusting herself to speak. She turned away quickly.

'Good night, Mr. Kendrick.'

And he let her go without another word.

Jim Kendrick's mistrust in her ability, his obvious rejection of her as a doctor, indeed, even as a woman, hurt her more than she cared to admit.

It's just because you're tired, she told herself fiercely, but knew it not to be the truth.

Katharine did not tell Anthony of her meeting with Jim nor of the distress it had caused her for he seemed irritable and on edge that evening.

'You're late, Katharine. How is she?'

As she told him, Katharine noticed that he moved restlessly in his chair and glanced angrily at his bandaged foot.

'Is it paining you, Anthony? Shall I re-bandage it for you?'

'No, yes, you can massage it a little, if you would.'

'It's the inactivity that's boring you,' she said as she unwound the bandage.

'You're right. I shall go mad sitting here. Can't I get out into the garden again tomorrow?'

'Should you, if it's hurting so much?'

'Perhaps not,' he replied gloomily.

Mrs. Rigby entered at that moment.

'Shall I set a supper tray for you, miss, seein' as you missed dinner?'

'Yes, yes, of course,' Anthony snapped, before Katharine could speak.

But Mrs. Rigby was undaunted. She folded her hands and stood before him.

'I hear Grannie Banroyd be reet bad, sir. 'Tis a shame you can't get to see her.'

Anthony looked up at her swiftly.

'If she had called Dr. Harvey earlier, she could have received as good attention as I could give her.'

Mrs. Rigby sniffed and glanced at Katharine disparagingly.

'Besides, Dr. Harvey has now taken her some medicine which I normally give her anyway,' Anthony added reluctantly.

'Mrs. Ford, down the road from Grannie Banroyd, says it's a far worse attack this time.'

'Then why,' Katharine broke in, 'didn't she send for me earlier and let me help her?'

Mrs. Rigby glanced at Katharine again, sniffed, and left the room.

Katharine sighed.

'She doesn't have to say a word and yet I know exactly what she's thinking,' she murmured sorrowfully. 'And if Grannie Banroyd does not recover . . .'

'She's an old woman, Kate, and suffered for years with bronchitis. Mrs. Rigby will come round in time. All the villagers will.'

'Well, I doubt I shall be here that long.'

'Won't you Kate?' There was a silence between them.

'I like having you here,' he added impulsively. 'Kate . . .'

'Yes?'

'Kate . . . would you . . . I mean, I know you've got the chance of this job in London, but how would it be . . . what I mean is, would you stay here?'

'How . . . how do you mean?' Katharine's heart beat a little faster. She was almost afraid of what Anthony was going to say.

He looked away from her.

'Well, the villagers will get used to you in time, and we could have a good partnership here, Kate. There's more than enough for one doctor.'

'But not enough for two practices, Anthony, you know that.'

'What I mean is . . . I'm not very good at this sort of thing. What I'm trying to say is . . . will you marry me, Kate?'

'Anthony!'

'Don't you see? I'm not trying to stop you being a doctor. I could help you. You're so marvellous with children and . . .'

'Anthony, please. Is this a business proposition or a proposal of marriage?'

'Oh, hang it all, Kate, you must know how I feel about you, I . . .'

'No, Anthony, don't, please don't. I'm sorry, but the answer is no.'

She was unprepared for the hurt in his eyes. She had not understood that his lack of declaration of affection for her was only through shyness. She could see from his face that he cared more than he had found it possible to put into words. For an educated man he was strangely inarticulate.

The subject was not spoken of between Katharine and Anthony again, but often she found him watching her and the look in his eyes told her that he was indeed very fond of her.

But two days later, all thoughts of Anthony's proposal were pushed from her mind. Grannie Banroyd died.

Katharine was at the cottage when death finally came. At the first sign of cardiac failure, Katharine had given Mrs. Banroyd a stimulant, but to no avail.

The child, Louise, became hysterical and, as soon as she was able, Katharine left the hovel taking the girl with her. Louise clung to her with one hand and with the other rubbed away the tears, which coursed down her sallow cheeks. Katharine led her away from her home and all the sadness it held. In the street, they turned in the direction of Dr. Stafford's house for Katharine could not allow the child to remain at the cottage and she knew of nowhere else to take her.

The front door of the cottage next to the Banroyds' opened and a woman stepped out, barring Katharine's way. She was a plump woman, her grey hair drawn back from her plain, round face into a tight bun. She stood with her arms folded. Her dress, far too tight for her rotund form, was dirty and crumpled. On her face was a similar expression to that Katharine had seen on Jim Kendrick's face – one of hostility and distrust.

'Tha'd best be leavin' t'lass with me, miss.'

Katharine stopped and hesitated, uncertain what to do for the best. Though the child would be cared for at Anthony's house for the present, it was an arrangement which could not last indefinitely. Perhaps, she thought quickly, it would be better for Louise to stay with these people, whom she knew to be called Ford. There were two Ford children, who were Louise's playmates and the child would find more comfort in less strange surroundings.

'Thank you, Mrs. Ford. I will.'

She released the child's hand and gave her a gentle push towards Mrs. Ford. 'Stay with Mrs. Ford, Louise dear. You'll be more at home.'

The child broke into fresh sobs and ran to Mrs. Ford, clutching the woman's skirts.

'There, there, my love,' Mrs. Ford said, patting the straggling, unruly curls. Above the child's head her eyes met Katharine's.

'Tha'd best leave her with me – tha'll not wish to be bothered.'

'It's not that,' Katharine retorted sharply, 'but I thought she'd be happier here with you – with people she knows.'

The woman smiled, but without humour.

'That's reet. We looks after our own, miss. We don't need no int'ference from outsiders. Besides, a fat lot o' good you done yonder.'

And she jerked her head sideways towards the Banroyd cottage.

What was the use in arguing, Katharine thought, as she walked on. Grannie Banroyd was dead and could not be brought back to life. The villagers blamed her. And yet the old woman had been over eighty, Katharine knew, but still they would blame her – the doctor who, just because she was a woman, could not be expected to be of use in such a crisis.

There was no more she could do. The undertakers arrived and Katharine's work, little as it had been, was done, and ill-done, according to the villagers.

The day of the funeral was chill and dull. Katharine watched the procession from the drawing-room window of 'The Sycamores'. The long line of people, all the village folk, it seemed to Katharine, wound down the narrow street and up the hill to the small church. Louise marched along behind the coffin. A pathetic figure, instructed, no doubt, to walk thus as chief mourner. But watching her, Katharine could not help but feel that it was a deliberate move on the part of Mrs. Ford to emphasise the small child's loss and to point a finger at the cause of her loss – Dr. Katharine Harvey.

'It's hopeless, Anthony,' she said in utter dejection. 'I'll never be accepted as a doctor – anywhere.'

Anthony packed his pipe with slow, methodical movements.

'It'll pass, Kate,' he said slowly. 'You're not one to give up a fight. You've nothing to reproach yourself about in Grannie Banroyd's case, you know that. It's only prejudice.'

'But what I can't understand,' she said turning away from the window and the sad spectacle, 'is Jim Kendrick's attitude. One would imagine him to be above such prejudice. I mean he . . . well . . . he seems so strong and reliable in most ways, that his injustice to me seems so out of character.'

Anthony puffed at his pipe and blue smoke drifted upwards.

'It's not only you. He's blaming me for bringing you here, and himself for not insisting that the doctor from the next dale visited Grannie Banroyd.'

'Doubtless *that* doctor is a man?' Katharine said bitterly.

'Naturally,' Anthony murmured. 'Jim's an odd one for sure and takes a lot of understanding. As I told you before – it's because of his mother. I suppose because boys tend to idolise their mothers – far more than girls do – such a betrayal of his love and trust comes hard to take. And Jim's a man of deep emotions, too, which makes it far worse.'

'I don't think he feels anything now. He seems hard and totally *un*feeling to me.'

Anthony laughed.

'Don't you believe it. He's like an iceberg, one-ninth on the surface and eight-ninths hidden from everyone. It only needs something to happen to change his outlook on life and in particular with regard to women and – wham – he'll be married with a dozen children in no time.'

Katharine, despite her depression, smiled at Anthony's psychological analysis of Jim. But she could not wholly shake off her disquiet and that night when she lay in bed, devoid of sleep, the moorland wind moaned in the trees outside her window, reminding her vividly of Grannie Banroyd's frail figure moaning softly in the neglected cottage. And the wind blew into a storm which lashed the valley in fury, for Katharine symbolising the anger of the villagers against her.

The days passed after Grannie Banroyd's death. Louise, Katharine learned, was being cared for by the Ford family – at Jim Kendrick's request and with a little weekly monetary assistance from him.

Katharine had tried, during the time Grannie Banroyd had been so ill, to visit Tommy Gifford again, only to be met by Mary, anxious as ever.

'I'm sorry, miss, but Tom says you're not to come again. And little Tommy's much better, really he is.'

There was no more she could do. Katharine had turned away without a word, sick at heart.

And now, after Grannie Banroyd's death, she found the villagers shunned her completely. Not only did the surgery remain empty, but they would not even acknowledge her presence as she walked down the street. Only Jim Kendrick, although he was the prime cause of her being avoided but less ill-mannered than the rest, spoke to her. And then he merely passed the time of day, his brown eyes holding hers in an intent gaze for a moment, before he moved on.

'I might as well return to London, Anthony, for all the good I'm doing here,' Katharine said frequently.

'Nonsense, Kate. Besides, I like having you here. Please stay.'

'All right.'

But she acquiesced against her better judgement, and two weeks later she regretted heartily that she had stayed in Brackenbeck at Anthony's request. Indeed, she bemoaned the fact that she had ever come to this dale.

And again Jim Kendrick was the cause of her chagrin.

Chapter Three

It was now July and the days were long and hot, even here on the moors which usually, because of their height and bleakness, remained comparatively cool.

There had been no rain for weeks – since the storm on the night of Grannie Banroyd's funeral. The ground became hard-baked and cracked through lack of water. The shrubs and plants withered and died. In the dale it was still and unbearably hot.

Anthony became ill-tempered with his enforced inactivity and was further irritated by the heat. His ankle was taking far longer to recover than he had anticipated.

'If *only* I could take a good, long walk over the moors, I'd be all right,' he said testily.

'I know, I know,' Katharine tried to sooth him, and walked over to the long windows to look out over the valley to the moors beyond.

'Anthony,' she said suddenly. 'What's that smoke?'

'Smoke! What smoke? Where, in heaven's name?'

Impatiently, he twisted round in his chair, so he could see out of the window.

'Look,' Katharine pointed. 'Up there, on the moor.'

'Oh my God, it's a moor fire. Quick, Kate, you must run and tell Joseph, the blacksmith. He's in charge when it comes to fires. Quick now.'

And Katharine ran. Out of the house, down the path, over the bridge and along the village street, her heart pounding, her breathing laboured. She neither knew nor cared whether the village women folk eyed her flying undignified figure with derision. This time, perhaps, when they learned her errand, they would thank her.

But perhaps not, she added to herself.

She neared the blacksmith's and heard the clanging of his huge hammer.

'Joseph, Joseph,' she panted, for Anthony had not told her the man's surname. 'Quickly there's a fire. A fire on the moors.'

Immediately the hammering ceased and Katharine was nearly knocked over by the robust blacksmith, who sprang from his work and out into the street yelling to his two workmates as he did so.

'Edmund, get t'farmers. Lad,' this to a young boy, 'get thee to t'quarry and tell master Jim. Look sharp.'

And the three of them disappeared in different directions leaving Katharine to lean against the door post to regain her breath.

Within seconds the once-deserted street was alive with scurrying figures: men hurrying to help extinguish the flames; children running to join in what they considered to be excitement, whilst the women chased the children to prevent them endangering themselves.

Katharine hurried back to the doctor's house to collect her medical bag, for she feared there would be burns, if nothing worse, requiring her attention.

She was delayed a few moments by Anthony's agitated questioning and advice, neither of which she wanted at that minute.

She was anxious to be gone.

Katharine left the village and began to climb the rough track in the direction of the fire. Now she could see a long arc of flames on the skyline. Thick smoke drifted skywards in heavy folds, and black ash floated everywhere. The acrid smell of burnt heather and bracken reached her making her eyes smart and causing her to cough. But she hurried on towards the fire.

She saw that the men had organised themselves into a line and were advancing steadily, beating the flames, their arms rising and falling rhythmically. Katharine pressed on, though the heat was becoming more intense, even though she was still a good distance from the fire. How could the men stand such heat? Whatever misunderstandings she had with the villagers, she could not help but admire the strength of character of these people.

Katharine could recognise some of the beaters now. There were the local farmers, Joseph, the blacksmith, and several men she knew were quarrymen, amongst them, she noticed, Jim Kendrick and his brother-in-law, Tom.

To her left, another figure appeared, climbing the hill towards the moor fire like herself. A tall, middle-aged man with a small, neat grey beard and carrying a black medical bag. Another doctor here, she questioned?

The man had seen her and came towards her now. He waved his hand in greeting and as he neared her, Katharine saw he was smiling. But the smile did not reach his eyes, which were pale blue and cold.

'Ah, you must be Dr. Harvey?'

'You have the advantage of me, sir,' Katharine said, for some inexplicable reason immediately on her guard against this man.

'Dr. Summers is the name,' and he gave a mock bow. 'I'm from the next dale. Mr. Kendrick sent for me. He saw the fire from the quarry before the alarm was given in the village and sent one of his men immediately to fetch me. Ah, there's Mr. Kendrick now, he's seen me. Pray excuse me, Dr. Harvey.'

Katharine remained motionless as Dr. Summers moved away to meet Jim Kendrick, who had detached himself from the line of beaters and was coming towards them. She was stunned by Dr. Summers' words.

'Mr. Kendrick sent for me.'

They hammered at her brain, '. . . sent one of his men immediately to fetch me.'

And the full impact of the insult to herself hit her. She did not know which she felt the most, anger or injured pride.

Jim and Dr. Summers exchanged a few words, then, whilst the doctor moved off towards the fire itself, Jim came to speak to her.

'It was good of you to come,' he was saying. 'And I understand you raised the alarm in the village, but Dr. Summers will take care of anyone who requires medical attention.'

Katharine stood before him, feeling hot and tired after her climb. And now she felt foolish beneath the gaze of this paragon of a man.

Her anger died and only the hurt remained, threatening to overwhelm her. She could not bring herself to speak. Her eyes met his momentarily and she knew she could not hide the mute appeal in her own. An appeal for understanding and acceptance. But rather than face further shame, she turned away quickly and stumbled down the hill.

She thought she heard him call her name faintly.

'Dr. Harvey,' but she did not look back and on later reflection decided she must have imagined it for he never acknowledged her as 'doctor'.

Almost in a bemused state, Katharine found her way back to 'The Sycamores'. Mrs. Rigby was hovering in the hall as Katharine entered the front door.

'Dr. Summers taken charge, I expect,' the housekeeper remarked.

Even in her present state, Katharine glanced at the woman in surprise.

'How did you know?' she blurted out before she could stop herself.

'Word gets round, miss,' Mrs. Rigby said, with a triumphant gleam in her eyes.

'It most certainly does,' remarked Katharine bitterly and entered the drawing-room, slamming the door behind her.

'Kate – back already? Why, Kate,' Anthony added, his tone changing as he saw her face. 'My dear girl, whatever is wrong?'

'Wrong? You may well ask! In two words I'll tell you – Jim Kendrick.'

'But . . .'

'He sent for Dr. Summers – instead of me.'

'How do you mean? How could he, we saw the fire first from here?'

'No, we didn't. It seems they saw it from the quarry too, and, to quote Dr. Summers, "Mr. Kendrick sent one of his men immediately to fetch me".'

'Oh dear.'

'That does it, Anthony. I'm leaving.'

'Now, Kate, you can't leave now. What shall I do?'

'Send for Dr. Summers,' Katharine replied with sarcasm, finding now that her natural resilient spirit was reasserting itself.

'But, Kate . . .'

'But, nothing. I'm going.'

'No, please don't go. You haven't had word about St. Bernadette's yet. Please stay, even if you don't look after my practice any more, stay and cheer me up. Please, Kate.'

And Anthony, exerting all his charm, managed to raise a smile from her.

'All right – all right. But I will *not* attend these villagers, if they come on bended knee.'

But her vehement declaration was to be proved meaningless. The devotion of a doctor for those in need of care was to prove too strong against even the fury of a scorned woman.

During the days which followed the fire, Katharine avoided any contact with the villagers and remained at 'The Sycamores' as a mere guest. She heard from Anthony, via Mrs. Rigby, that on the occasions when a doctor was needed, Dr. Summers was required to make the toilsome journey across the moors to Brackenbeck.

Anthony's ankle, though much improved, still did not enable him to return to his practice and for the most part, fortunately for Dr. Summers, the people of Brackenbeck remained in remarkably good health.

Until one August afternoon when Katharine and Anthony were enjoying a leisurely hour in the garden. Anthony had once more hobbled the short distance from the house to the garden seat. It was the first time since the moor fire that they had been able to sit in the garden, for the day after the fire, as if in ridicule, the fine weather had broken and the rain had alternated between heavy downpours or continuous light drizzle for over a week. But now, though the ground was still sodden, the weather had brightened, and it was fine and quite warm.

Katharine had put on her prettiest afternoon dress of blue

shantung with lace trimmings. Her hat was straw with velvet ribbon trimming.

Katharine and Anthony were deep in conversation on a recent development in medicine, when the distant sound of a deep rumble, which seemed to last an inordinate length of time, disturbed them.

'Whatever was that?'

'I should think it's from the quarry,' Anthony replied and their eyes immediately sought the skyline in that direction.

Silence followed – a deathly silence.

Then the villagers, who could not help but hear the sound, came running from their houses. Katharine and Anthony from their vantage point on the hill could see them converge in the street and exchange conversation. From this distance they could not, of course, see the anxious faces nor hear the worried questions – but they could guess the fear which surrounds every community whose men are engaged in dangerous work.

With one accord the villagers began to hurry up the hill: wives and mothers, their children clinging to their skirts; the older men and young boys not yet employed at the quarry. And immediately, Katharine saw, the farm hands too were hurrying from the fields on the hillsides in the direction of the quarry.

'Kate . . .' Anthony began.

'I'm on my way,' was her reply and, with all thought of the incident of the fire driven from her mind, she ran towards the house to fetch her medical bag, pausing only to collect a few instruments and a good supply of dressings.

Most of the villagers were ahead of her by the time she reached the road leading up the hill and over into the quarry. It was a long twisting track and all the more arduous because of the fear which dwelt in their hearts.

Above them three men appeared at the crest of the hill and began to hurry down towards them. Katharine saw the villagers quicken their pace towards the men, eager for news.

There could be no doubt that something disastrous had happened.

Katharine's breathing became laboured, she was unused to

climbing at such a pace. Her heavy skirts hampered her progress and her black bag became a leaden weight.

The two parties had converged and the tale was being told, but Katharine could not yet hear. She saw one of the boys turn and run back down the hill towards her.

'Dr. Stafford, Dr. Stafford,' his cry reached her ears. 'I'll get Dr. Stafford.'

'No, Dr. Summers,' one of the women called after him.

Katharine hurried on again, her lungs bursting. The boy flew down the track towards her and would have passed her had she not stopped him. 'What's happened?'

'Accident at the quarry. Mr. Jim and Mr. Tom is trapped, probably kill't.'

And he ran on, determined to fetch someone he thought could help.

Katharine turned her face towards the waiting knot of villagers who, their eyes following the running figure of the boy, had now seen her coming. Katharine tried to run as best she could, and breathless, she reached them.

She saw the naked distress in their eyes and she saw too that still they thought she could not help them.

'Why are we wasting time here?' Katharine asked, and without waiting for a reply she marched on up the hill.

The men from the quarry fell into step beside her.

'There's nowt thee can do, miss.'

'There might be.'

'There be only a narrow tunnel down, miss, none of us can get right through. Luke got so far, but there's a reet narrow piece where a huge rock's fallen and left such a small hole none of us could get through,' said another. 'We'll have to dig them out.'

'It'd take days,' muttered a third.

'Can you hear anything of them?' Katharine asked calmly.

'Ay, ay, we have,' the first man, whom Katharine knew as Luke said. 'Jim can get as far out as the other side of this big rock we've been telling you about.'

'Are they badly hurt, do you know?'

'Jim says – Tom's leg's badly smashed up.'

'And Jim?' Katharine felt her heart beat faster. No doubt it was a tiring climb.

'He says he – mind you, he's not one to complain – he says he's just hurt his arm.'

'We'll never get them out,' moaned one of the men.

'Nonsense,' said Katharine swiftly. 'They're alive. You must.'

'Of course we must,' said Luke. 'Don't talk so soft, George.'

'Are there just the two of them, no one else at all?' Katharine said.

'That's right,' said Luke, who was obviously the senior man now that Jim and his brother-in-law were absent.

'See, miss, they goes in to set the explosive. No one else is allowed to do it, because of the danger.'

'Do you mean they were still in there when it went off?' Katharine asked in alarm.

'Nay, nay, they were setting it when the sides of the tunnel gave way behind them. They're in no danger from the explosive itself.'

'But plenty from the rock. That tunnel where they are could go any minute,' said the pessimistic George.

'Oh no.'

A woman's wail behind them made them all turn. Mary Gifford had heard most of their conversation. The anguish on her face was pitiful. Though the whole village was concerned, only she would bear the double grief if the two men could not be rescued. Mrs. Johnson, a kindly middle-aged woman, whom Katharine knew by sight, put her arm about Mary's shoulders.

'Now, now, lass, they'll get out, never fear.'

They came to the top of the hill and Katharine saw before her for the first time, the quarry around which the lives of most of the villagers revolved.

The twin arms of the two cranes, silhouettes against the sky, formed, by accident, an ill-omened cross.

Katharine felt Luke's hand on her arm.

'This way, miss. O'er t'judd wall,' and she gave him her hand as he helped her over the wall which surrounded the brink of the quarry.

'Now down huggers' ladder, miss. Reckon you'll manage it, d'thee?'

'Yes, if you'd be good enough to take my bag. Thank you.'

And Katharine lowered herself down the ladder with very broad rungs set closely together.

Soon she was standing with Luke at the bottom of the ladder, the quarry sides towering above her. The stone, she noticed briefly, was cut out in huge steps, like a giant's staircase. The village women climbed down the ladders without assistance and the children, with a mixture of the fear and yet delight in the unexpected visit to the quarry, swarmed all over.

The villagers, though they still disbelieved her ability to help them, now no longer seemed to resent her presence. They reached the part where the work had been going on, and here several more men stood or knelt at the small opening which was obviously the tunnel where the men were trapped.

'What actually happened, Luke?' she said, looking at the cliff-like rock face and then at the heap of smaller, broken rocks before her.

'Well, see there was this long passage-like gallery, see through there,' he pointed, 'open to the sky, you see. We'd been quarrying along this particular seam, y'see, for some time. Then we comes to this massive piece and Jim wanted to get it out as big as he could for a big millstone needed over Halifax way. He decided to go in and set small charges the size he wants the stone – to crack it away, like. That were going all reet, but,' he pointed skywards. 'Us reckons there must have been a fissure in t'rock and the sides decides to cave in reet this minute.'

'But didn't Jim *know* they were unsafe?'

'They've been safe as houses for weeks, miss. It's the rain we've had, weighted it, it did. Does tha see?'

Katharine was not sure she did, but her job was not an enquiry into the accident but to get to the injured men. Again she looked at the fall of rocks. Miraculously, a small tunnel had been left when the rocks fell. Though the tunnel had been blocked in several places at the start, Katharine learnt, Luke had been able to remove all obstructions until he had come up against a massive piece of rock which could not be moved. It would take them hours to dig the two men out, for the narrow part of the tunnel was a long way in, near where the two men were trapped, and long before that Tom's leg would need attention. Unattended for such a length of time, it could easily result in the subsequent loss of his leg.

Katharine knew she must at least try to reach the injured men. The hole left by the fall of rock may still be too narrow even for her, but she must try to get through.

But she knew something else too. The danger to herself was great.

'Here,' she said to Luke. 'Tie a length of rope to my bag.'

'What are thee about, miss?'

She looked at the creased face of the middle-aged man before her.

'I'm going to them, of course.'

'But thee canna. 'Tisn't safe.'

'Mary,' Katharine called. Mary Gifford came forward, the tears coursing down her cheeks. Mrs. Johnson moved forward too, her arm still comfortingly about Mary's shoulders.

'Be brave, Mary, they'll get them out. Here, I need your help. Ask the ladies to stand round me, will you, whilst I take a few of these bulky petticoats off, and will you take them for me?'

'We'll help thee, miss, if tha can do anything,' Mrs. Johnson said.

Katharine's suggestion was carried out swiftly and with no argument from the women. They seemed stunned by the accident and Katharine's calm organisation met with no opposition from them.

But as she returned to the tunnel opening, George spoke.

'Thee'll be kill't as well, miss. Thee canna go.'

'I can and I will,' Katharine said calmly. 'There's not one of you can get through, and if you got there, what could you do?'

Luke scratched his head.

'I don't like it,' he muttered. 'Jim wouldn't like it.'

'Jim's not here to argue the point,' Katharine said. 'I take full responsibility. There'll be no blame on anyone else, only on myself. Now Luke, will you be good enough to tie the rope round my waist so that my bag is pulled along after me as I crawl in.'

George knelt down by the tunnel, whilst Luke tied the rope around Katharine's slim waist.

'Jim can you hear me?'

A distant murmur was heard.

'The lady doctor reckons she can get to you?'

'No.' The bellow came distinctly. 'She's not to be so foolish.'

'But Tom's leg, what about it?' shouted George.

There was silence.

The waiting villagers could feel Jim's agony. He needed medical attention for Tom and yet he could not entertain the idea of a third person being endangered too.

'She's not to come,' came the reply after a moment, presumably when Jim had consulted Tom.

'George, will you please move out of my way,' said Katharine, still maintaining the calm tone of voice.

'You heard what he said,' began Luke.

Katharine turned, her eyes flashing.

'Luke, there are injured men in there. I am, whether you will acknowledge it or not, a qualified doctor. I pledged my life to save others. Now will you allow me to get on with trying to do so?'

The villagers remained silent and watchful, whilst Katharine knelt down and wriggled into the hole.

The darkness ahead as she moved forward engulfed her as the last glimmer of light was blotted out by her own body. The tunnel was painfully narrow. Sharp stones threatened her every movement and soon her scalp tingled as her head kept hitting the top of the tunnel, whilst her elbows were chafed and became painfully sore. Her shoulders ached with the effort and she began to sweat, whether from the exertion or fear of the enclosed space, she knew not.

Slowly and painfully she moved forward. She could see nothing but blackness, could hear nothing but her own difficult breathing and the scraping sound of her movements. Her medical bag bumped along behind her, at times catching against a rock and pulling at her waist so that the rope felt to be cutting her.

'Are thee all right,' came a faint shout, but whether it was from those behind her or from Jim in front, Katharine could not tell. She paused.

'Yes,' she panted, and again louder in case they had not heard. 'Yes.'

Then without doubt from ahead came Jim's voice.

'Miss Harvey, you're to go back. I command you to go back.'

Katharine though far from feeling happy, could not help being amused at the arrogant authority in his voice.

'There's no – going back, Mr. Kendrick – sir.'

And again she moved forward.

Again Jim was shouting to her, but unless she kept still, her movements drowned his faint voice, and she chose to ignore his orders.

It seemed hours that she continued in this way, like some terrible nightmare when she wished to wake up and find it all unreal.

But it was all real, painfully real. She reached the part where the tunnel became so narrow and here were her worst moments. The space left by the rock looked ridiculously small even for her slight frame. She squeezed herself into the small aperture and for a time it felt as if she were buried alive. Panic was all too near, but just as she felt she could bear the pressure no longer, the tunnel widened again.

'Are you all right, Miss Harvey?' Jim's anxious voice was quite near now – blissfully near.

'Yes, quite, thank you.'

On and on she crawled. A glimmer of light appeared ahead. Suddenly, without warning the tunnel stopped and opened out into a small cave. And at once Jim's strong arms were helping her from the tunnel and lifting her upright. What bliss it was to stand again.

The light from a small lamp shone full on her face as she smoothed her dress and began to tug at the rope around her waist.

'Miss Harvey, Katharine . . .' Jim's voice was deep, his hands still on her shoulders. 'You shouldn't have come.'

'Well, I'm here now. Let me look at Tom.'

Katharine had already seen the figure lying in the shadows on the far side of the small cave-like hole in which Tom and Jim had been saved from a worse fate. Jim's strong, yet gentle, fingers untied the rope and he held her bag for her.

Poor Tom was writhing in agony and moaning softly. Katharine knelt before him and swiftly her gentle hands moved expertly over his body searching for broken bones. All was well until she came to his right leg. The dim light showed her the torn trouser leg soaked with blood and when she gently pulled back the cloth it was to reveal a sickening sight of blood, and torn flesh, but miraculously, no broken bone.

She heard Jim draw a sharp breath. But to Katharine this sort of sight was nothing new. She had seen many such sights, and worse, in her training. Her one thought was to do the best she could in the dreadful circumstances of poor light and dirty conditions to save Tom's leg. The wound was ugly and painful and sepsis was a grave probability from all the dust and dirt in the wound.

'He's lost a lot of blood,' Jim said softly.

'Yes – but it's as well in a way. It's nature's way of cleansing the wound of much of this dirt. But I'm afraid there's still a lot we've got to get rid of. Jim, can we not get any better light?'

'I'll try, but we wanted to save it as much as possible.'

He held the light as near to Tom's leg as he could.

'That's better. Hold it there, will you? Tom, I'm going to put a tourniquet on your leg, well above the wound and then raise your leg, to try and stop the bleeding, so that I can work on the wound.'

Tom, obviously in considerable anguish, merely nodded.

This done, Katharine turned to the wound itself.

'If only the conditions were not so hopeless,' she muttered to herself more than to the two men. Though she had intended that neither should hear her exasperation, especially Tom, it appeared that Jim, ever attentive, had not missed her words.

'I'm so sorry, Katharine but I can get no more light.'

'It's not that, Jim,' she reassured him quickly. 'It's not your fault at all, but without the ordinary facilities of cleanliness,' she spread out her own dusty fingers, 'let alone proper sterilisation of my instruments, I hardly like to start. However,' she opened her bag and took out a large bottle, 'this is a carbolic solution. If I wipe my hands and all my instruments with this, perhaps we may win.'

Katharine worked swiftly and gently, cleansing the whole area of the wound with gauze soaked in antiseptic lotion. On the bleeding points she applied pressure-forceps. Gently and cautiously, she untied the tourniquet and saw that the severe bleeding had been arrested. She then tied ligatures round the points held by the forceps. Finally, removing the forceps, she covered the whole wound with a gauze dressing, held lightly in place with bandages.

'It's bad, isn't it?' said Tom.

'It could be a lot worse,' she replied.

'It hurts like . . .'

'Like hell – go on, say it,' Katharine said. 'It'll help.'

She glanced at Tom's face and saw him grin weakly. It did him good, for immediately a little colour returned to his ashen face and he relaxed a little. Jim knelt beside her holding the lamp steadily, his eyes fixed on Katharine's hands. She felt, rather than saw, that he approved of her work.

'This is only just to keep any more dirt out until we can get you to hospital, where they can do a proper job,' she said as she secured the last bandage.

'I reckon tha's done a proper job, lass.' Tom said, and she could not fail to hear the surprise in his voice. 'It feels better already.'

'Good. Then try and get some sleep. They'll be a while getting us out yet.'

'Yes – Doctor.'

Katharine turned at his words and saw the sheepish grin on his face. Tom grasped her hand and squeezed it quickly.

'I'm reet glad tha come, lass. Thanks.' And he turned away in embarrassment.

Katharine too felt the same shyness, but coupled with a warm rush of gratitude to Tom for voicing his appreciation. She turned away and stood up. Jim stood beside her and they then moved away from Tom to the other side of the cave.

'How bad is it, Katharine? It looks dreadful.'

She could not help but notice his natural use of her Christian name and realised that she too had used his unthinkingly.

'Jim, I'm worried about it. I've done all I can do to stop infection in the wound and in doing so have given him temporary relief – though how he stood all my cutting and probing, I'll never know. But his nerves – though obviously of iron – can only stand so much. I'm very much afraid that when he wakes he'll be suffering severely from shock.'

'What can we do?'

'Well, the pain will be bad and if he starts to be restless and move about, he could undo what bit of good I have tried to do.'

'Katharine,' Jim said quietly, 'though I don't know much about being a doctor, I've sense enough to know you've done a grand job there.'

She smiled quickly, gratified by his words. Praise from Jim Kendrick – she had never expected to hear it.

'The best thing I can think of which would ease his pain and help the shock factor would be an injection of morphia.'

Jim ran his hand distractedly through his hair.

'How bad is the fall? How long are they likely to be?'

'It seemed miles coming here, I can tell you. It'll be a long while before they can clear it all – too long, I'm afraid.'

'Then – then what can we do?' he said helplessly.

'I'll try and shout to them down the tunnel and ask them to go to Anthony for what I need – then if they get it here, I'll go and fetch it.'

'Katharine, you can't go down that tunnel again.'

His hands gripped her shoulders.

'It's bad enough you being *here*,' he added, 'but the tunnel is even more dangerous.'

'Jim,' Katharine said softly. 'Please try to understand. I had to tell Luke the same thing to let me come. I've dedicated my life to being a doctor and, therefore, to my patients, and right now Tom's my patient.'

Jim let his hands fall from her shoulders and he sighed heavily. She saw him wince in pain.

'It's time I had a look at your arm.'

'It's nothing.'

'Come on, Mr. Kendrick, sir.'

And with a smile he gave way.

Swiftly she examined his left arm and found that although there was no bone broken, it was badly bruised and sprained. She made a rough sling and fastened it round his neck. As she did so, he slipped his right arm about her waist. 'Katharine, thank you for what you've done, for Tom and – me.'

In the dim light, she looked into his dark brown eyes and saw the unspoken apology for his previous behaviour. An apology for all the occasions when he had refused to accept her as a doctor, and she knew that foremost in his mind was the incident of the moor fire.

He seemed about to say more, but Katharine prevented him. She was not the kind of woman who wished to see the pride of a man like Jim Kendrick crushed. She did not demand his humiliation. Katharine had read the humble apology in his eyes and that was enough for her.

'Think nothing of it,' she said lightly.

'I think a great deal of it, Katharine. More than you could guess.'

A moan from Tom interrupted any further conversation. An examination of the injured man told Katharine that the time had come, sooner than she had thought, for her return through the tunnel. Tom's forehead was covered with beads of sweat and again he was tossing in pain.

Katharine went to the small opening of the tunnel.

'Luke,' she shouted.

'Yes,' came the faint reply.

'Is Dr. Stafford there?'

'Yes. The lads have carried him down, miss.'

'Good – can he hear me?'

There was a pause, then Anthony's voice echoed down the tunnel.

'I'm here, Kate.'

'Anthony, have you any morphia with you?'

'Yes.'

'Good, I'm coming for it.'

She turned back to Jim.

'Anthony's managed to get here and has brought the very drug I need. I'm going to fetch it.'

'Is it really impossible for *anyone* else to get through?' The worried frown on his face was deeper than ever. He ran his fingers through his thick, dark hair, glancing first at Tom and then back at Katharine in helpless anguish.

Impulsively, Katharine put her hand on his arm.

'Yes, it is. Don't worry, I'll be right back.'

And in the faint light from his lamp, she smiled up at him. But there was no answering smile in his dark eyes. His huge hand covered hers briefly before she drew away and knelt down ready to enter the tunnel.

'Katharine – take care.'

But already her head and shoulders were in the tunnel and she was concentrating on the ordeal ahead. Never would she admit it, but this journey up and down the tunnel was sheer torture for Katharine.

She had always feared enclosed places and now she was experiencing her severest test ever. Her progress was agonisingly slow and painful. At times she heard the shouts of those at either end. Jim called frequently and Anthony too, now he had reached the mouth of the tunnel, kept enquiring on her progress. It was comforting and yet, at the same time, annoying for each time someone called she had to stop to listen whilst they repeated it and then answer. And shouting for her wasn't easy, for her breathing was laboured with the effort of wriggling and pushing herself forward.

At length a glimmer of light appeared ahead, and with the upper earth in sight, her heart lightened considerably. She dared not think of the return journey at present.

Luke helped her from the tunnel, stiff and cramped as she was. She found it had taken her longer to come back than to get to

Jim. Luke had timed her in an effort to ascertain how far the tunnel stretched to the trapped men.

'How far do you think it is, Doctor?'

Katharine started in surprise at the use of the unfamiliar address, but she showed no sign on her face.

'Luke, I'm terribly bad at gauging distance and especially moving like that. It seems miles, but it can't be, of course.'

'I reckon it must be about thirty yards,' Luke said.

'Is that all?' Katharine said, sitting down on a rock and rubbing her shoulders.

'It takes a lot of crawling through, Kate,' said Anthony soberly, 'and a lot of digging to get them out.'

There was a silence amongst the waiting people. Katharine looked round for Mary Gifford.

'Mary,' she said as she spotted her amongst the villagers, still clutching Katharine's clothes under her arm.

'Mary, come here,' and as the girl neared her, 'don't worry too much about Tom. His leg's not so bad, especially when I get back with this drug. It'll kill the pain for him.'

Mary nodded, the tears springing to her eyes.

'You're reet brave, Doctor, I – I–' and the tears flowed more as she choked over her words.

Katharine understood what she was trying to say and patted her arm.

'It's no more than anyone else would do, if they could but get through,' Katharine said softly for Mary's ears alone, though she feared Luke was standing too close to miss her words.

'It's time I went back,' Katharine said brightly now and louder. Cheerfully, she took the package that Anthony held out to her.

'The morphia is in the hypodermic syringe all ready, Kate, and I've packed it as best I can to prevent breakage.' He grinned, but without much of his nonchalance. Anxiety sobered his buoyant gaiety.

The journey back down the tunnel was even worse than Katharine had feared. Black despair engulfed her. She had to grit her teeth and force herself back into the tunnel. Only the thought of Tom's wound, and Jim waiting for her, made her leave the open air far behind. She could not shake off the fear that she may never see the sun again.

Already the men were making steady progress digging away the fall of rock and, in fact, she had some four yards less to crawl through on her return than when she had first gone into the tunnel.

Every movement was a pain. The sharp rocks were like knives. The tunnel roof threatened to collapse and the darkness suffocated her. The dust, rising as she moved, choked her, forcing her to stop. But when she did, fear of being trapped was greater so that she moved on, still coughing. Her eyes ran, her skin prickled with fear and her mouth became lined with dust. Her dress was torn and her fingers bleeding, but she held the package carefully, trying to think of nothing but Tom and Jim waiting for her.

'Katharine, are you all right?' Soon she heard Jim's voice floating out of the darkness.

Her heart lifted.

'Yes. I'm coming,' she shouted. 'I have the drug. I'll soon be there.'

And with fresh vigour derived from his encouragement, she pushed ahead.

Again, she saw the dim glow from Jim's lamp. He had lit it, she felt sure, to welcome her back, for she knew he wanted to preserve the light for as long as possible. But the use of it was not wasted, for its glow transmitted warmth to Katharine's fearful heart.

Her hands were already reaching out towards the end of the tunnel when she heard above her an ominous rumble growing louder. Frightened, she tried to hurry. Distantly, she heard Jim's shout.

'Katharine – Katharine, hurry – the tunnel.'

The earth cracked above her and just as she was about to crawl out of the tunnel, and even as Jim's arms reached to help her, she felt a tremendous weight upon her back crushing her.

She cried out in anguish.

Chapter Four

The tunnel had collapsed seconds before she would have been free and Katharine was trapped from the waist down to her feet.

She felt waves of sickness pass over her as the pain shot through her body. She willed herself not to faint and tried to concentrate on Jim. He knelt before her, his voice husky with anguish.

'Oh, Katharine, I should have pulled you clear, if only – oh my God, what a mess.'

'Jim – Jim,' she gasped, full realisation hitting her. 'The package – where is it?'

'You dropped it on the floor.' He bent to pick it up.

'It's here. It's all right – not broken.'

'Tom . . .' she started to say, but Jim interrupted her.

'I'm getting you out first.'

'Jim – you must – give it to Tom.'

'But, Katharine . . .'

'*Please*, Jim. I'll tell you what to do.'

Dimly, she saw Tom struggle to sit up on the far side of the cave.

'Jim – Jim, what's happening,' he called, his voice muffled and tremulous. She knew instinctively that he was racked with pain and fever, barely conscious of the happenings around him. He must receive the medication immediately.

'It's Katharine, she's trapped by a fall, just as she got back,' Jim replied.

'My God – is she – all right?'

'Fine, Tom, just fine,' Katharine tried to call brightly. 'Jim,' she added urgently, 'get that injection into him, will you?'

'What injection?' Tom asked, as Jim moved reluctantly across the cave towards him.

'It's the drug I went for, Tom. It'll kill the pain for you.'

'No – I don't want to now, Katharine. You must have it, it'll help you.'

'Don't–' she paused and gasped as fresh pain surged through her body, threatening to engulf her. 'Don't be silly, Tom. It's nothing that can help me. Now be a good chap and take it, or else it'll all have been in vain.'

Jim came back and knelt beside her and took her hand in his.

'Let me try to get you out, *please?*'

'No,' she said far more firmly than she felt, for the panic at being trapped welled up in her and she had to bite her lips not only to stop herself from crying out in pain but to prevent herself from begging Jim to get her free as quickly as possible.

Reluctantly, Jim turned away and knelt beside Tom. In calm tones Katharine explained to him how to give Tom the much-needed injection. She watched with admiration in the dim light as Jim's hands, with unexpected gentleness and deftness, administered the morphia. He was a man of character, she mused, forgetting for a moment her own pain.

Her task of instruction completed, she shut her eyes and allowed herself a soft moan. Unfortunately, Jim, returning to her, heard her and immediately began to reproach himself for obeying her instead of trying to free her first.

'I should not be wasting time. Katharine, I should . . .'

'Nonsense,' she said opening her eyes again and willing herself to keep her groaning in check.

Jim began methodically to dig away the rock around her with his bare hands. Though he worked quietly and calmly, Katharine knew he held himself in check with great effort. She felt, without him saying the actual words, that his natural reaction was to tear frantically at the rocks to free her. She warmed to him for this feeling for her. But his common sense told him, she knew, that by so doing he would probably only make matters worse.

The pain in her back grew worse. The whole of her spine seemed to be on fire, and beads of sweat broke out on her forehead. She tried to concentrate on Tom's condition. She asked Jim to take his pulse, to feel his head and report to her on his general colour. Tom himself was sleeping now and Katharine felt this to be the best thing. Her journey had not been in vain for without the injection he would have been conscious and in terrible pain. She only wished that she herself were unconscious too, instead of suffering as she was now.

Patiently Jim worked to free her whilst she concentrated on biting back the groans which rose naturally to her lips. His anxious eyes told her that he was not ignorant of her suffering. He worked until his breath came in painful gasps, until at last he had, even with his great strength, to take a moment's rest, leaning heavily against the rough rock.

At last he was able to give her some hope.

'Katharine, there's a huge piece of rock resting on your back. The only way I can get you out is to hold this up, whilst you struggle free.'

'I – don't know whether I can move, Jim,' Katharine said in all truthfulness.

He took her hand in his.

'Try, Katharine, just try. I can't hold t'rock and you as well.'

She nodded.

'I'll try.'

Jim braced himself and eased the rock from resting on her, his strong fingers torn by the jagged edges, his muscles straining to their utmost.

'Right,' he gasped.

Katharine tried to pull herself forward with her hands. Her legs were numb, there was no feeling from her waist downwards at all.

'Go – on,' Jim commanded.

Katharine grappled with the floor of the cave, her fingers feebly clutching for something on which to pull herself forward. Inch by inch her arms pulled the leaden weight of her useless body forward. With agonising slowness, Katharine moved forward whilst all the time Jim stood, like Hercules, above her holding up, Katharine thought, a ton of rock.

At last, she was clear and thankfully Jim eased the rock back into place carefully so that more rock above would not be displaced too quickly to come crashing down to engulf all three of them. He turned to Katharine and knelt by her side. He was breathing heavily, but there was a triumphant look in his eyes. At the sight of her face, Katharine saw the look die and anxiety return.

'My dear girl – is it – very bad?'

His kindness threatened to overwhelm her and she felt dangerously near to tears. She must not let him see her weep, see her weakness now. She merely nodded and bit her lip.

'There's nothing you can do,' she said anticipating his next words. 'It's maybe – not as bad as it feels.'

'I pray to God not,' Jim said in his deep tones.

'Please, have a look at Tom now.'

Jim moved across the cave.

'He's still asleep. Looks a much better colour, and,' he said, putting his hand on his brother-in-law's forehead, 'he's not so hot.'

Katharine closed her eyes, thankful that at least all her efforts, and her own injury, had not been in vain. It sounded, from Jim's heartening report, as if Tom was going to be all right.

How long she slept, she had no idea, but Katharine woke to the blackness of the cave and a stabbing pain in her back. Fear threatened to overwhelm her, but then she remembered Jim was with her.

She tried to sit up, but found it impossible.

Her movement must have aroused Jim, for immediately the light illuminated the cave and his anxious face was bending over her. 'Katharine, are you all right?'

'I think so, but I can't move.'

'What?' His question was a whisper, full of fear.

'I can't feel my legs and I can't sit up.'

'My God,' his voice was hoarse.

Immediately, Katharine realised his anguish, which, for some reason she could not now understand, far exceeded her own.

'It'll be all right, it's just – temporary, I should think,' she added, willing it to be so.

Jim did not answer, but in the dim light she could read the disbelief on his face.

He feared the worst, she could see, and blamed himself.

'Listen,' Katharine said suddenly.

Distantly, they heard the tap-tap sound of the rescuers.

'They must be getting very near now,' she said. 'How long is it, how long was I asleep?'

'About twelve hours.'

'Twelve hours! I slept all that time? How's Tom? You should have woken me.'

She twisted her head trying to see Tom.

'Lie still. Tom's all right. He roused round once, said he felt a lot better and dropped off again.'

'You should have woken me,' she repeated.

'You needed the rest.'

Now she saw for the first time the dark shadows beneath his eyes. This was a terrible ordeal for Jim Kendrick. It was his quarry. His own brother-in-law was badly hurt and now he had her injury on his conscience as well.

'Jim,' she said hesitantly. 'Jim, I want you to know that what has happened is in no way your fault. You're not to blame yourself. I came of my own free will to attend an injured man. What has happened to me I brought about myself.'

'Luke should have stopped you.'

'He couldn't – apart from forcibly holding me. And you couldn't expect him to do that.'

'You would not have come if I had been up there.'

Even through the pain, Katharine could smile.

'The conceit of the man! You'd have, had a fine fight on your hands, I can tell you, Jim Kendrick.'

The sounds of their rescuers grew louder. Soon they heard Luke shouting.

'Jim, you there Jim?'

'Ay, Luke. You're not so far off now, lad, but go easy or you'll have the lot down on top of us.'

'We'll mind it.'

There was silence in the cave as they listened to the sounds of the workmen. The chipping of the rock followed by the scraping of shovels as they carefully cleared away each portion. What an endless task it was for them, Katharine thought. How tired they all must be. Now that help was near, she forgot some of her pain in listening to the progress they made. A light shone into the cave from the rescuers' lamps.

'What are they doing, Jim? How have they reached us?'

'I imagine they've had to dig it all away up as far as that big stone, then perhaps they've just made this last piece of tunnel larger, probably shoring it up as they go along.'

Pieces of rock began to fall into the cave and Jim leant over Katharine protectively.

At that moment Luke crawled through the narrow hole and stood up in the cave. He looked around and took in the situation at a glance, Katharine knew. She also guessed what was in Jim's mind. So forestalling him she said,

'Please take Tom out first. He needs medical attention urgently.'

'No, Katharine . . .'

'Please do as I ask?' she said firmly.

She heard Jim sigh.

'Katharine, you will be taken out first, whether you like it or not.'

There was no more she could do. Jim's word was law and whilst she was helpless she had to obey him. Gently Jim picked her up in his arms. Luke scratched his head thoughtfully.

'I don't quite know how we're to get her out, master Jim. We've only made a narrow tunnel this end. Didn't like to waste no more time making it larger, besides the risk o' further falls.'

'Have you any blankets?' Jim asked.

'Yes the women have brought dozens up.'

'Good, get about three, we'll make a sort of sling.'

Luke turned back into the tunnel. In the few moments he was

gone, Jim made no move to put Katharine down again. He stood there with her in his arms, looking down at her.

'You're as light as a feather, lass.'

Katharine noticed his lapse into the Yorkshire dialect – unusual in Jim. She brushed a wisp of hair from her eyes.

'I must look ghastly,' she said knowing she looked white and drawn after all the pain, which even now stabbed constantly in her spine.

'Tha's–' he paused the compliment coming awkwardly, 'beautiful.'

The word was a whisper so that she hardly heard it and later was to wonder if she ever had.

Jim and Luke wrapped her in the blankets using the third as a hammock-type of stretcher. Carefully they entered the tunnel, now considerably shorter than when Katharine had crawled through it on her own. Luke took one end of the blanket and Jim the other. The tunnel was much larger now, but even so, it meant that the two men, especially Jim with his giant proportions, had to crawl on their hands and knees and in some places, where they had been unable to enlarge it much, Luke was forced to wriggle out backwards and Jim forwards, both on their stomachs. Katharine, although wrapped in the blankets, was bumped and bruised however carefully the two men tried to move her. It was an impossible task to do otherwise.

As they emerged the villagers clustered round, their chatter in a lighter, happier tone now that they knew their men would soon be safe.

Anthony was to the forefront, and was soon stooping over Katharine.

'My dear Kate, what have they done to you?' His voice was hoarse with emotion and Katharine felt the surprise of the villagers as their chatter died away, their eyes directed towards the two doctors and also Jim who knelt on the other side of Katharine.

'The tunnel fell on her just as she got back to us . . .'

Anthony's face reddened.

'And could you do nothing?' he said between his teeth, his blue eyes, usually so jovial, flashing in anger.

'Jim did everything possible, more, if truth be known, than could be expected,' Katharine said weakly.

'I'm sorry, Kate,' said Anthony swiftly, 'arguing here when we should be getting you home – but,' he turned back to Jim. 'I'm not through with this yet.'

Jim turned away, but not before Katharine had seen the hurt in his eyes. After all, he looked upon Anthony as his closest friend. Jim Kendrick already blamed himself, not only for the hurt suffered by Tom, but also for Katharine's injury.

Jim and Luke disappeared down the tunnel again, and Anthony gave orders for Katharine to be carried to his house. He must wait for Tom to be brought out, he explained to her, but he would return home as quickly as possible. Anthony had already arranged, it seemed, for Tom to be taken to the cottage hospital in the town some ten miles over the moors. It would be a painful journey and a cold one for it was now early morning.

As the village menfolk carried her up the steep ladders of the quarry and down the track towards the village, Katharine could not help but admire their devotion and single-mindedness for their small community. All the men, she was sure, and a good many of the women-folk as could be spared away from young children, had spent the night either in the quarry itself or making frequent trips between the village and the quarry carrying blankets and warm drinks to the workers and watchers.

Soon she was back at the house and laid carefully on the bed. With great difficulty and no little pain, she undressed and rolled beneath the covers. Mrs. Rigby, unbending from her aloof manner, helped her.

''Ave they got Tom out, then?' she asked.

Katharine nodded.

'Yes, but his leg's badly injured.'

'Will 'ee lose it?'

Katharine marvelled that in her impatience for news of Tom Gifford, Mrs. Rigby forgot herself sufficiently to ask Katharine's opinion.

60

'I hope not,' she answered soberly. 'But the delay in proper attention will not have helped, I fear.'

Mrs. Rigby sniffed.

'I s'pect there wasn't much you could do when you got down there, miss.'

'I did my best,' replied Katharine, and closed her eyes. She was too exhausted to be angry or hurt.

Mrs. Rigby left the room and Katharine fell into a restless sleep disturbed by racking pain and fear that the injury to her back might be exceedingly serious. Before, she had not had time to dwell on the fact. Her attention had been on Tom, her patient. But now, with Tom safely in other hands, the possible magnitude of her own injury began to assert itself. As she drifted again towards sleep, her last thoughts were of Jim. The strong, masterful Mr. Kendrick, but for whom she would most likely still be pinned down beneath that awful rock. She smiled in spite of the pain as she thought of his last command, when he had overruled her and brought her out first. Master of all he surveyed, undoubtedly . . .

When Katharine awoke, the sun was high in the sky. As consciousness returned, so did the pain. Anthony rose awkwardly from a chair near the window and hopped towards the bed.

'Now, Kate old girl, we'd better have a look at that back. Do you want Mrs. Rigby in whilst I examine you?'

'Of course not, Anthony.'

After a thorough examination, Anthony said:

'There doesn't seem to be any serious damage done, no broken bones. The pain you're getting is probably bad bruising and temporary muscle dislocation.'

Katharine sighed with relief.

'The pain feels better already now you've told me that.'

'You'll have to rest for a few days . . .'

'What about Tom?' Katharine interrupted.

'Everything's fine there. He'll be laid up a long, long time, but with a bit of luck, he won't lose his leg. Thanks to you, I might add.'

She smiled sheepishly.

'It's no more than anyone would have done.'

'It's a great deal more than a lot of folk would have done, Kate my dear, and now, believe it or not, the villagers realise it too.'

'They do?' Katharine could not keep the surprise from her voice.

'They want you to stay, Kate,' Anthony said softly.

Katharine twisted her head away and frowned.

'Anthony, please, you know I have vowed to dedicate my life to medicine.'

She heard him sigh but he did not speak and it was not until she heard the door close softly that she realised he had left the room, had given up the fight and was letting her have her way.

Dear Anthony, she thought, he was a good friend and she was fond of him as such, but she could never love him with the passion she anticipated one should feel for a man with whom one wanted to spend life. The man she would give her heart to, she mused, would be of a much stronger, sterner character than Anthony. A giant of a man, who would quell even her rebellious spirit.

And unbidden, the face of Jim Kendrick flashed into her mind.

Katharine slept.

After three days in bed, Katharine was anxious to be up and moving about.

'Please let me get up, Anthony?'

'I think you should stay where you are another day or so, Kate.'

'The pain's much easier, really. I feel the exercise would be the best thing now.'

Anthony grinned.

'All right, Dr. Harvey. Have your own stubborn way.'

But he succeeded in extracting a promise from her that the drawing-room chaise-longue was to be the extent of her travels and there she would remain until returning to bed.

'We look a pretty pair of physicians, I must say,' Katharine remarked as she settled herself comfortably on the sofa and looked across at Anthony now sprawled again in his leather armchair, his injured ankle resting on a footstool. He was dressed, as ever, in comfortable country clothes. His blue eyes twinkled back at her merrily through the curling blue pipe smoke. He certainly did not appear to be suffering the pangs of unrequited love on account of her refusal to marry him.

'Much faith we shall inspire in our patients, eh?'

At that moment Mrs. Rigby entered.

'Mr. Kendrick is here, sir.'

'Ah,' said Anthony with expression. Katharine noticed immediately that his face lost some of its expression of jollity and solemnity shadowed his eyes.

For a moment she could not understand, but then with sudden clarity, she knew.

Anthony and Jim had presumably not met again since their encounter in the quarry and Anthony still held Jim responsible for the accident involving Katharine.

'Anthony . . .' she began, but at that moment Jim came into the room and further conversation between herself and Anthony was impossible. Instead Katharine smiled brightly at Jim, whose eyes had immediately sought her on entry. Katharine prayed silently that Anthony would follow her lead, but it was not to be, for before Jim or Katharine could speak, Anthony said,

'Ah, Jim. Come to see the damage you've caused . . .'

'Anthony,' cried Katharine, 'that's unjust and you know it.'

'Let Jim defend himself. He's never needed to shelter behind a woman's skirts and not likely to start now. Well, Jim?'

The two men faced each other angrily.

Then suddenly the anger died on Jim's face, his shoulders slumped and he sat down heavily on a nearby chair.

'You're right, of course, I must take full responsibility.'

Katharine could almost have laughed, if the moment had not been so serious, at the incredulity on Anthony's face.

'You do? Well – er – I'm glad to hear it. What do you propose to do about it?'

Jim spread his hands helplessly.

'What can I do? You tell me and I'll do it.'

'Er – well – um,' Anthony rubbed his chin. Then Katharine allowed herself to laugh, relieving much of the tension.

'Come on, you two. Acting like a pair of schoolboys. There's nothing to be done.'

But the worried frown on Jim's face would not be laughed away.

'You must have the best medical attention, of course, and anything I can do to compensate . . .'

'Say no more about it, I shall be as fit as ever in a day or so,' she replied, with far more conviction than she felt.

Anthony sighed and then grinned sheepishly.

'Well, I suppose if Kate is prepared to acquit you of all blame, I must do the same.'

'I shall never forgive myself, though,' Jim said softly, his sober eyes on Katharine's face. Katharine laughed, though not unkindly.

'Nonsense, in a few months when I'm back in London, you will have forgotten all about me.'

A startled look crossed Jim's face and he looked first from Katharine to Anthony and then back to her face.

'You're leaving? But I thought – the villagers thought . . .'

'Thought what?' Katharine asked.

Jim shook his head.

'It doesn't matter. I thought you'd be staying. Now, especially.'

'I don't understand,' she said.

'It doesn't matter,' Jim repeated, so Katharine changed the subject.

The three of them talked for some time about the village life, about the country's situation in general and the increasing popularity of the motor car.

'I think I shall have one eventually, perhaps when they've improved upon the design a little,' Jim said.

'It would be a remarkably useful object for a doctor,' mused Anthony. 'But I'm sure the price in my case would be prohibitive.'

'I see you agree with progress then, Jim – mechanically, that is,' Katharine added with meaning.

He had the grace to laugh.

'You insinuate that there are matters in which I do not like progression?'

'Women doctors, for example,' she said mischievously.

'I'm rapidly changing my mind on that point,' he said quietly, his eyes smiling in a way she had not seen before on the usually solemn face of Jim Kendrick.

'Jim was the first in the district to install the steam crane at the quarry, Kate.' Anthony said.

'But didn't the villagers object? I always thought that the country folk hated change of any sort and mistrusted these new inventions.'

'They do – to a certain extent. But I was lucky in first having established a good relationship with my men, and discussing it fully with them beforehand. They felt that they had been consulted, you see, that their opinion mattered.'

'Come off it, Jim, they eat out of your hand. If you told them they could fly like birds if they jumped off the top of the quarry, they'd do it,' Anthony laughed.

Jim laughed too.

'Not quite as bad as that, I hope. I've no desire to become a dictator.'

Jim called several times during the course of the next few weeks and an easy relationship developed between Katharine and Jim. Anthony, Katharine thought, looked upon their friendship with growing concern. Whilst he did not entertain the idea of Katharine involving herself with Jim, he obviously felt that Jim was rapidly becoming fonder of Katharine than was wise.

'Don't string him along, Kate.'

'Anthony, really! You make me sound a regular Jezebel.'

He smiled wryly.

'You underestimate your own feminine powers, my dear, so intent are you in competing in a man's world.'

She was silent for she could think of no retort.

It seemed the whole village were following Jim's lead, and were trying to make amends for their previous behaviour. Mary visited her carrying a huge bouquet of flowers from the villagers. Katharine was undoubtedly their heroine now.

'We'll never forget what tha's done for us,' Mary said shyly.

'Oh Mary, it was no more than anyone would have done had they been able.'

'We think it is, doctor.' Mary's soft voice, so gentle and shy, held a note of firmness. But Katharine wished that it had not taken a tragedy to win over the people of Brackenbeck. She had far rather they accepted her for her own self and not just because she had shown bravery. However, she was thankful that their opinion of her had changed, whatever the instrument of change had been.

A few mornings later, Anthony, his ankle now much improved allowing him to take up his duties once more, came into the dining-room at breakfast time, holding a long, thin envelope in his hand.

'This has arrived for you, Kate, from London.'

With trembling fingers she opened it and read with excitement that she had been accepted as a doctor attached to the children's wing of St. Bernadette's hospital in London. It was the appointment for which she had longed.

Day by day she grew stronger and her back ceased to pain her so much.

The day before she was due to leave Brackenbeck, she walked down to the village to say goodbye to the Giffords, to the other villagers and to Jim Kendrick.

Her welcome at the Gifford household was exuberant. Tom, home now from the hospital, was the centre of the household. From his bed in the small living-room, he ran the life of the home. Young Tommy romped by, on and under his father's bed, whilst Mary looked on with her adoring, gentle eyes.

'Tha's not leaving us, now, lass, surely?' said Tom.

'There's no reason for me to stay here, Tom. And I've obtained the appointment in London, which I wanted.'

She saw Tom glance at Mary, saw the latter shake her head slightly, and was puzzled. Tom cleared his throat.

'Jim wants to see you. Tha's not going without seeing him?'

'Of course not,' she smiled. 'When will he be home from the quarry?'

'He's home now.'

'In the middle of the afternoon?'

'He didna want to miss seeing thee. We thought thee might call today.'

Tom did not look at her so she could not see if he were telling her the truth. Cold fear washed over her. Was Jim ill, injured in the accident worse than she knew?

She rose from her chair hardly noticing the twinge of pain in her spine.

'I'll go now. Goodbye, Tom, Mary and little Tommy. I'll see you again some time, I'm sure.'

Tom nodded.

'Ay, we hope so.'

His grasp was warm and strong. 'Maybe sooner than you think,' he murmured.

Katharine smiled and left. Next door the smoke curled from the single chimney. Katharine knocked on the brown painted door. Jim opened it, his shoulders bent slightly to adjust to the height of the doorway.

He smiled and for a fleeting moment the frown left his face.

'I've come to say goodbye, Jim,' Katharine said.

The frown returned swiftly.

'Katharine, will you walk with me up the dale? Are you strong enough?'

'Why, I'd love to, Jim. I've seen all too little of the countryside during my stay.'

The air was clear and sharp as they left the village far behind and climbed slowly up the slopes of the dale. Higher and higher until the village was far below them, looking as it had on Katharine's first sight of it. They hardly spoke as they climbed, except when Jim pointed out some difficult piece of ground, giving her his hand in support. Most of the time he was silent, his eyes on the ground, as if lost in his own thoughts.

So his sudden question startled Katharine.

'Are you going to marry Anthony?'

She stopped in surprise, and looked up at him. His deep brown eyes looked down at her as he towered above her.

'Whatever makes you ask that?'

'The villagers said from the start that you must be going to be married, with you staying there ...'

'I'm sorry if it offends your idea of propriety,' she laughed.

'It's not that,' he looked hurt and was silent.

'No, I'm not going to marry Anthony. I'm going back to London. I have obtained a post in the children's wing of a big hospital. It's what I've always wanted.'

'For how long?'

'How do you mean?'

'How long will you stay there?'

Katharine shrugged.

'As long as they want me, I suppose.'

'But you can't go for good, I mean, you must come back.'

'Here?'

'Yes.'

'Why?'

'Because – Katharine ...' he stopped again and turned to face her, taking her slim shoulders in his hands.

'Because I love you, Katharine, I want you to marry me.'

For a long time, it seemed, they stood staring at each other, Katharine in bewilderment, Jim, anxious, now hiding none of the deep emotion he felt. She saw plainly in his face the extent of his feeling for her. This was no idle fancy, this was no gratitude mistaken for love, following the accident.

'But why?' she whispered. 'I thought – I thought you disliked women.'

His grip tightened, drawing her towards him.

'No, Katharine, I just did not want to fall in love. I didn't believe in it. But now, I can't help myself. Me,' his tone was incredulous, 'helplessly in love with a slip of a girl.'

He drew her to him and bent his head to kiss her. There, high on the hillside, with only the sky and the birds as witness, he declared his love. And as he kissed her, Katharine felt herself respond.

Suddenly she broke away as passion threatened to overwhelm her.

'No – no, Jim. It's no use.'

She turned away and began to run down the hill.

'Katharine, Katharine,' his voice bounced over the breeze.

Tears blinded her as she rushed on heedlessly. She tripped and stretched out her hands helplessly. But his strong arms caught and held her, and she clung to him. But her words belied her action.

'I can't marry you, Jim, I can't.'

'My darling Katharine, why not?'

'Please try to understand. I've dedicated my life to medicine. I've vowed. They've given me years of training. They extracted my promise that I would never waste it.'

As he threatened to protest, she laid her fingers gently against his lips.

'Don't you see? I cannot allow myself to fall in love. I cannot love you Jim, I am not free.'

'Katharine, you cannot mean it, you cannot be so blind, so stubborn. No one can hold you to such a promise.'

Katharine shook her head slowly. ·

'You wouldn't be asking this of a married woman, Jim. You wouldn't ask this of a nun, who is married to the Church. Then can't you understand that I am married to medicine?'

Anger darkened Jim's face.

'You cannot be serious, Katharine?'

Katharine sighed.

'I am. Maybe in twenty or thirty years' time a woman will have the right to have a career and marriage as well. But through man's blindness and stubbornness, a woman is supposed to sit at home all day and let life pass her by.'

'Her life should be her husband and children.'

'For some, perhaps. But why should not those with the ability contribute something to this world? It's not so perfect, run by men, that it couldn't do with improvement.'

Jim was silent. His grip on her shoulders relaxed and his arms fell loosely to his sides. He turned away. Katharine caught at his arm.

'You do understand, Jim?'

He shook his head and said slowly,

'I understand only that you don't care for me.'

'I'm not in a position to *allow* myself to care – for anyone. If I did – then – then it would be for you,' she added softly.

He turned back swiftly.

'Then let yourself care, Katharine, dearest.'

Tears blinded her again at the ardour in his voice. Her heart cried out against the rejection of the love he offered.

'Do you want to spend your life alone?' Jim said softly.

Katharine's chin hardened.

'It was my choice. It was no good sitting around waiting for a man who might never come. I did not think I would ever fall in love – or – or be loved.'

Despite the gravity of their conversation, Katharine saw a small smile play at the corners of his mouth.

'You are the most lovable creature I ever knew.'

He made to pull her to him again, but Katharine resisted, afraid that she would give way beneath the power of this man.

'Katharine, Katharine,' Jim's voice was hoarse. 'Have I to beg you?'

Katharine shook her head.

'My answer's no, Jim. It must be, and will be.'

They returned from the hillside in silence. They reached the village and Jim escorted her to Anthony's house.

He turned to face her at the gateway.

'Then that is your final answer?'

She nodded, afraid to speak.

'Very well,' he said, his voice flat and emotionless now.

Jim Kendrick turned and walked away and Katharine watched him out of sight.

But he did not look back.

The next morning, she left Brackenbeck early. Anthony wanted to take her over the hill to the station, but she told him she preferred to go alone. For some reason, she wished to leave the valley as she had arrived. On foot and alone.

She was passing through the village as the quarrymen were leaving for work. Their good wishes echoed in her ears. Their exhortations to 'come back soon, doctor' were proof of her final conquest over their initial antagonism. But still her heart was heavy and her feet taking her away from the village were like lead.

Jim emerged from his cottage, and stopped when he saw her only a few yards from him. They looked at each other. Katharine went to him.

'Jim I'm sorry. Please try to understand and forgive me?'

At first he did not answer. She could not read the expression on his face. The frowning mask she had seen on her arrival in Brackenbeck was back, his eyes unreadable depths.

Where was the love that only yesterday had shone from his face?

He shook his head slowly.

'I cannot,' he said.

Slowly, she turned and walked down the cobbled street away from him. She climbed the long hill out of the village. But before she lost sight of Jim's cottage, she turned round. He was still standing just as she had left him, watching her out of sight.

She lifted her hand in farewell, but there was no answering wave from him. He could not forgive her.

Katharine left Brackenbeck and Jim Kendrick with bitterness in his heart.

Chapter Five

Five long years passed after Dr, Katharine Harvey left Brackenbeck. Five years in which the outward life of the village continued in much the same way as it had done before her arrival. Tom Gifford did not lose his leg, though it was stiffened and he walked with a slight limp.

He and all the villagers, however, were not ignorant of the fact that he owed his life to the girl who had bravely attended to his injuries.

But not all was the same.

Jim Kendrick was a changed man. On the day Katharine had left, he had watched her out of sight and even then had stood staring at the point where she had finally disappeared, before he turned back into his cottage and shut the door. He did not come out of the cottage for over a week and during that time, Mary, his sister, was the only person who saw him and knew the depth of his suffering. He was unshaven and sleepless, not eating, just sitting in his small parlour, speaking to no one.

But this Mary kept to herself and though rumour and conjecture were rife through the valley, Mary knew that the village folk had short memories and would soon forget. Jim never talked about Katharine nor told Mary what had happened between them, but his sister guessed and was sorry. She had grown fond of Katharine, respecting and admiring her, and would dearly have loved her as a friend and sister-in-law. Mary, a shy, gentle girl, did not make friends easily and was often lonely for another woman's company.

But her heart also held anger against Katharine for distressing her beloved brother so. But she felt herself helpless for she had not the resolve to interfere.

For several months after Katharine left Brackenbeck, the villagers talked of her and asked Dr. Stafford for news of her. But word soon passed round, as word will in a small community, that her name was not to be spoken of to Jim Kendrick. Over the months the villagers' interest waned. Other happenings, both domestic and national, superseded the quarry accident.

Life continued.

Anthony Stafford heard infrequently for the first year from Katharine by letter. And he answered cheerfully enough. But somehow their letters were stilted as if each were avoiding a particular subject – a painful subject.

And in truth they were. The subject being Jim Kendrick. He could not forget her, even though he was probably the only one of the community who particularly wished he could do so, and yet found it an impossibility.

Anthony and Jim were gradually restored to their former friendship though there was a slight reserve on either side, some withdrawing of old confidences. For between them lay the ghost of Katharine's presence. Neither spoke of her from the time she disappeared over the hill, and yet, whenever they met, she was there in their thoughts.

Jim returned to the quarry for a few months and worked with a feverish intensity and yet his outward appearance was one of cold reserve, hard as the rock he quarried. The men, respecting him, said nothing.

Some six months after Katharine's departure, Jim was called to his dying father's bedside and before the old man died, father and son were somewhat reconciled. On his father's death, Jim found himself heir to a considerable estate, far more than he had imagined the old man had amassed. He became owner of three more quarries and much of the farmland surrounding Brackenbeck, which, though unsuitable for arable farming, was reasonably valuable in parts for grazing.

The quarry held bitter memories for him and Jim was relieved to have the excuse to cut himself off entirely from it. He made over the four quarries to his sister as her share of their father's estate. The old man had been stubborn to the last in remaining estranged from his daughter. But Jim, of course, saw that their shares were equal.

He opened up Kendrick House, redecorated and renovated it. For Mary and Tom, he built a similar house on the quarry side of Brackenbeck valley, on the opposite hillside to Kendrick House.

But in Kendrick House, Jim lived alone and lonely. He took up various interests: sheep farming, grouse shooting and still he maintained an interest in the motor car. From London came reports that the horseless carriage had reached twenty miles per hour, and at the same time the suffragettes were causing much talk and speculation. The world was changing from the narrow confines of the Victorian era. Jim, against his will, searched the news of the suffrage movement for Katharine's name, but failing to see mention of her presumed she was far too preoccupied with her medical work to join the women pioneers.

It could be supposed that Jim Kendrick's action in taking advantage of his new-found wealth caused a rift between himself and the villagers. Far from it. The affection and respect of the people of Brackenbeck were so deep-rooted that not one would say other than that had they found themselves in the very same position they would have done exactly the same as Jim. Besides, they were not forgotten. Any word of hardship or suffering reaching Jim's ears concerning one of the village folk, did not pass by without action on his part. Whether money or help was needed, neither was found wanting in him. Though Jim lived now more the life of the gentry – a life which was his birthright, for only the estrangement from his father had caused his former hardship – he was still a villager at heart and in mind. He took care that no elderly inhabitant suffered as had Grannie Banroyd, in poverty and loneliness. He remembered the shame and remorse he had felt when he had learnt of the suffering the old lady and her grandchild had borne: how in his prejudice he had blamed Katharine for the woman's death, when in fact he might have helped in a positive way earlier.

Never would such a thing happen again now that he had money at his command, Jim resolved.

Five years passed after Katharine left Brackenbeck. Five long years. Jim, at length, bought his motor car and never was the contraption seen chugging along the rough, hilly roads round Brackenbeck, but that dozens of village children were packed into it. If Jim did not get his full measure of enjoyment from it, there was little doubt but that the children did.

But in spite of all this, Jim Kendrick remained a lonely man and though time is supposed to lessen a hurt such as he had suffered, he found that with him it did not. Whatever interest he undertook, it was never enough. The memory of a bright-haired girl, so neat and beautiful was seared in his mind and on his heart.

Mary and Tom Gifford produced another offspring – a little girl, tiny and delicate, who grew to be the favourite of her uncle. At three she became Jim's constant companion and whilst Mary teased her brother that she never saw her own daughter, secretly she rejoiced that he found some comfort in the small child's company.

But was it because the small girl was so delicately formed and so pretty, with red curls and dancing dark eyes? Or because they called her Kate?

Anthony at last acknowledged to himself that though he had been very fond of Katharine, his affection for her was infinitesimal beside Jim's love for her. They could have been happy, Anthony thought, but their marriage would have been based on a good friendship and a mutual interest in medicine, rather than the 'grand passion'. He admitted to himself that he had been wrong in having proposed at all, and that it was his pride, and not his ardour, which had suffered the blow of her rejection.

Unlike Jim, time cured Anthony of such thoughts concerning Katharine, but they did not erase the memory of her friendship nor the knowledge, though no words passed between them, that his friend Jim suffered torture every day of his life because of her. And whilst he watched Jim build his new life, watched him reopen Kendrick House and make it a home, all the time Anthony wondered if Jim nurtured the hope that Katharine would, in time, return to him, and that all this was in preparation for the day when she would become his wife.

But the years passed with no word from Katharine. And Jim Kendrick remained alone and lonely in his grand house.

And so when Anthony had to attend a conference in London during the summer five years after Katharine's visit to Brackenbeck, and found that time hung heavily on his hands when the actual conference was not in session, he decided to seek out and learn for himself whether or not the plans she had had five years before had reached fruition.

It was a spur of the moment decision made on the first evening of his stay in London. The day's conference disbanded, his dinner at the hotel over, it was not yet eight o'clock on a fine evening and Anthony was bored. He remembered the name of the hospital to which Katharine had been appointed when she had left Brackenbeck, and knowing a hospital doors are never closed he took a hansom cab that very evening to 'St. Bernadettes'.

Once he had set his mind to it, he was impatient to see her again.

The huge hospital sprawled over several acres of land and the Children's Department alone was a maze of corridors and wards. The happy atmosphere was immediately apparent, the children's voices echoing with laughter down the corridors. Only the occasional sobbing of a child in pain or in fear reminded him of the reason they were here. He could understand Katharine's desire to be part of such an organisation, where such devotion was repaid a thousandfold by the recovery of the small patients.

With some difficulty he found the matron's office. She was not available and he had to wait over half-an-hour before she was free to speak to him.

'Dr. Stafford – from Yorkshire,' she said as she shook hands. She was a thin, spare woman with a capable-looking face and brisk manner, but her eyes were filled with compassion.

'Matron,' Anthony murmured. 'Thank you,' as she motioned to him to be seated.

She seated herself behind her desk opposite him.

'And how may I help you?'

'I'll not keep you, Matron. I see how busy you are.'

She smiled beneath his charm.

'I wonder if you can help me to find an old friend, who, I believe, is a doctor with the Children's Hospital here. Dr. Katharine Harvey. She came about five years ago . . .'

Matron had raised her eyebrows in surprise.

'Then you don't know, Dr. Stafford?'

'I'm sorry?' he murmured, puzzled by her words.

'Obviously not.' She sighed and spread her hands before her on the desk. She looked down at them as if carefully examining her fingers, but Anthony knew she did not want to look at him.

'Dr. Stafford, before I tell you about Dr. Harvey, may I ask you a very personal question? Please don't feel obliged to answer it, but . . .'

'Of course, what is it?' he said, impatient for the solving of this mystery.

'Is your friendship with Dr. Harvey of the – romantic nature?'

Anthony sighed and smiled ruefully.

'Not really, though I could wish it on my part.'

The matron relaxed a little.

'It will still, I fear, be a shock to you, Dr. Stafford. Dr. Harvey is a cripple.'

Anthony stared at her for a few moments, numb with shock. Her words seemed unreal. It was not possible.

'It seems she was involved in some kind of accident shortly before she took up her appointment with us . . .'

'Oh my God,' Anthony muttered, his usual composure shattered. He covered his face with his hands.

'You know about it?' The matron's voice was gentle.

He nodded.

'For over a year,' she continued softly, 'Dr. Harvey carried out her duties excellently. Then, one day when she was assisting the Resident Surgeon, she collapsed. I might add, that by this time, Dr. Harvey was completely accepted as a very able doctor, though,' she smiled, 'I'm afraid some of the men gave her a rough time at the outset. We tried all sorts of treatment and for a time there seemed hope of recovery. Several eminent doctors examined her, but finally, two years after she first took up her appointment here, it was obvious she could no longer carry on as a doctor. She could not, and still cannot walk.'

Anthony groaned. After a pause, his voice trembling slightly, he asked.

'Where is she now? In hospital?'

'No, unfortunately, space is not available to keep someone in hospital for whom nothing can be done. I'm afraid she lives in rather harsh circumstances. I'll let you have the address.'

She moved to a cabinet.

'And you say *nothing* can be done,' he asked.

The matron shook her head.

'Everything has been tried. But it seems there is some mystery as to the exact nature of the paralysis. They cannot seem to find what can be causing the paralysis. There are no bones broken, no lacerations of the muscles – and for it to happen so long after the accident is a further mystery. The nearest the doctors will diagnose is functional paraplegia, but really,' she shrugged, 'it is quite a mystery.'

'And is she completely helpless?'

'Oh no, only her legs are affected and even then, she can stand, but as soon as she tries to walk, her legs give way and she falls. I'm very sorry you've had to learn in this way. I was under the impression that Dr. Harvey was quite alone in the world.'

'Who looks after her?'

'She is a brave girl, Dr. Stafford. She does a great deal for herself from her bathchair. But a sister with whom she became friendly whilst here, goes regularly to help her.'

Anthony rose.

'I must see her.'

The matron wrote swiftly on a piece of paper and handed it to him.

'This is her address. Prepare yourself for the poverty of the neighbourhood, Dr. Stafford.'

Anthony left the hospital in a daze. He had decided to see Katharine on the spur of the moment, and now he had discovered that she was living in poverty, paralysed and alone, all because of her visit to Brackenbeck.

As he left the hospital, noticing that it was now half past nine, Anthony realised that he could not visit Katharine that night. He would have to wait for the morrow. His mind troubled with the knowledge he had so recently acquired, he decided to walk back to his hotel, although it was some three miles. Through the streets of London he strode, hardly noticing the tall houses on either side; the ragged urchins who jostled him shrieking and laughing; the hurrying folk on their way home; the grand carriages sweeping past him, taking richly-dressed ladies and fine gentlemen to grand dinners and balls. The horses' hooves clip-clopping, the rattling wheels of the carriages were only background noises. He was unaware of them. Only the picture of Katharine, a cripple, was vivid in his eyes.

What of Jim now? He walked on slowly, thoughtfully. What was the right thing for him, Anthony, to do? Was it his duty to remain silent for Katharine's sake or to tell Jim for his sake? Obviously, Katharine did not wish Jim to know or she would have let him know before this time. Or would her pride prevent her?

Anthony sighed. Here was a pretty mess, indeed! The morrow would decide him when he had seen her.

He spent a restless night and the day's conference washed over him without him hearing much or taking any part. He was impatient for the evening. He dined quickly and left the hotel immediately, having ordered a cab to be waiting for him. The driver was old and, so it seemed, was the horse, for their pace seemed lethargic to the impatient young man. Presently, they reached a poor area of the city. The cab driver stopped and, leaning down, asked,

'You sure you got the right haddress, young sir, it don't seem the right place for the likes o' you, I'm thinking?'

'No,' murmured Anthony, more to himself than to the cab driver. 'It's certainly no place for the likes of me, or Katharine.' He raised his voice. 'No, I'm sure this is the right place. Are we to the address I gave you?'

'Not quite, sir, but ha little further.'

They moved on down the grimy street. Children, thin and ragged, played in the gutter, squealing and shouting at each other, their pinched little faces lined with dirt. Besides these urchins the children of Brackenbeck looked like princes – pictures of health and happiness. The cab reached the tenement house where Katharine now lived. It was a grim street with a grey outlook. Anthony rang the doorbell and waited until a shabbily-dressed woman opened it to him.

'I'm looking for Dr. Harvey?'

The woman jerked her thumb over her shoulder.

'Down thur.'

He stepped into the dark hall. The door slammed behind him.

'Furst on yer right. 'As to 'ave a bottom floor room, she does. Crippled, she is.'

'Thank you,' he said curtly, not wishing to prolong the conversation. He knocked on the door and at the reply entered the room.

He had prepared himself for a change in the girl he knew. He had expected her to look ill – thin and pale perhaps. But he had not expected such a vast change in her appearance, in her attitude. Her skin was white, almost translucent. Her hair, pulled back into an unbecoming bun, lacked the lustrous auburn colour it had had five years before.

But her eyes held the greatest shock for him.

Gone was all the joy of living, gone was all the fight. And in its place was defeatism and bitterness.

Even when she saw him and tried to smile, the smile did not reach her eyes. Her eyes, which had once been so alive and warm and challenging, were now cold and empty.

'Anthony!'

'Katie, my dear girl,' he could not keep the smile fixed on his own face. It faded as he went towards her bathchair.

'Katie, why ever didn't you let me know?'

'How are you, Anthony?' she said, deliberately avoiding his question. 'You're looking well.'

So not all the fight had gone, he thought, or had it been replaced by an unnecessary pride? A pride which had prevented her from telling him, or Jim. Suddenly he realised he must not mention Jim's name to her. If he did, she would probably bind him to secrecy. And that he did not want, he knew now.

He took in the bareness of the room. He was relieved to see that it could have been a lot worse. Its sparseness of comfort tore at his heart, but at least it was clean. Katharine, seated near the window, although it looked out upon the narrow grimy street, was at least able to feel not quite so shut away.

'Kate, how do you manage? I mean . . .' he faltered, embarrassed.

'I make out. I have a small annuity left to me by my father and occasionally I write for a medical journal and a medical column in a daily paper.' She paused and the hopeless look flooded her eyes. 'They wouldn't let me stay at the hospital, Anthony. They said I couldn't do my work from a chair. They said I was – no use.'

Anthony took her hand as he sat beside her. What could he say? The only course of action open to him he could not discuss with her.

'We'll see what can be done, Kate.'

They talked a little longer about trivial matters. But there was an undercurrent of embarrassment between them and soon Anthony made an excuse to leave. He walked the streets back to the hotel again, instead of taking a cab.

There were two days of the conference left and Anthony must stay, impatient though he was to get back to Yorkshire. He tried hard to concentrate on his work, but it was impossible. His thoughts kept returning to Katharine, alone in her dingy room, and to Jim, alone in Kendrick House.

Of course, he must tell Jim. But what would come of it? Would Jim still want her now? Anthony believed he would. But would Katharine marry him? He thought not. Anthony sighed. But that was for Jim to solve, not him. All he could do was to put the matter into Jim's hands now.

The train back to Yorkshire was painfully slow, and never before had Anthony covered the distance between the small station and the dale with such swift strides. He took the same path which Katharine had taken on that first day coming to Brackenbeck, and, like her, he branched off the road leading down to the valley itself and up the lane leading to Kendrick House.

But now the house was no longer deserted. The lane leading to it had been cleared of undergrowth and gave evidence of constant use. As he neared the walls surrounding the house, Anthony could see through the wrought-iron gates the lights from the long windows of the house. True, it was no longer uninhabited, but still there was an air of loneliness about the place, as if it were waiting for something or someone.

Anthony paused at the gate, standing for a moment not only to gain his breath after his long, brisk walk, but also to collect his thoughts and to try and think how best to break the news to his friend. He walked slowly up the curving driveway and stood before the door. The heavy knocker fell against the door with a dull thud and Anthony waited, looking across the darkened lawn, for it was now late in the evening, and beyond the low walls of the grounds to the soft lights of the villagers' cottages.

Jim answered the door himself.

'Come away in,' he said when he saw who was knocking at his door. 'And how was the big, bad city?' he continued, attempting humour, though Anthony knew his joviality was limited and had been for five years.

'Jim,' Anthony said, pacing up and down the small room Jim called his study, after refusing to sit down.

'I've got some news for you, bad news.'

Jim poked the fire in the huge grate and the sparks flew, casting grotesque shadows about the room. He waited in silence for Anthony to continue.

'I suddenly took it into my head to look up Katharine,' Anthony said, and he turned to look at Jim.

He saw the look of pain flit across his friend's face, the tightening of his lips, the eyes become wary, defensive.

Still Jim said nothing.

'I went to the hospital where she took up that appointment when she left here.' He paused and the silence deepened. 'She's no longer there.'

He waited for some comment from Jim, some sign of interest.

Jim shrugged.

'So? She's moved on, no doubt, to promotion.' He jabbed viciously at a piece of wood with the poker.

Anthony shook his head slowly.

'That's just where you're wrong, Jim. She can't move on. She – can't move at all.'

Jim's head jerked up and his eyes sought Anthony's face anxiously.

'What are thee telling me, man?'

'Katharine's crippled. A helpless cripple in a bathchair in a godforsaken dump of a room.'

'My – God,' Jim breathed hoarsely. The poker slipped from his fingers and fell to the hearth with a clatter. Coal fell and sparks flew, but the two men paid no heed. They continued to stare at each other.

'The quarry accident, was that the cause?' Jim's voice was but a whisper.

Anthony shrugged.

'Indirectly, I suppose – yes. But her doctors have diagnosed something similar to functional paraplegia.'

'What on earth is that?'

'Paralysis, but not caused by physical disease, rather of the emotional kind. It usually follows suddenly on some fright or shock, or an injury even though the injury itself is slight.'

'But you're saying there's no *reason* for her paralysis. That it's all in her mind? Katharine's too strong a character to allow such a thing to happen.'

'Nothing of the kind. She is powerless against it as surely as if she'd broken her spine. There's no telling what may be the full explanation – eminent doctors in London have admitted themselves baffled and I would not presume to try to improve upon their diagnosis, but – knowing the full circumstances, which I am sure they do not – I would hazard a guess that the quarry accident, followed by an emotional involvement with you, has caused the trouble.'

'*She* wasn't emotionally involved with *me*,' Jim said bitterly.

'I think you're wrong there. She has fought against nature in smothering her emotions and Nature will not allow herself to be so thwarted.'

'Is there any possibility of recovery?'

'Oh yes, and it often happens quite suddenly and without warning and she would be able to return to her normal life. Then again, she has been like it now for almost four years, so . . .' he shrugged and left the words unsaid. Being a doctor he did not like to be pessimistic about recovery.

'Why,' Jim said softly more to himself than to Anthony. 'Why did she not let us know?' He shook his head sadly. 'She could have let me know.'

'Our Kate's got courage and a lot of pride, Jim.'

'It's my fault. We parted – in – in such – with such mis-understanding. She'll think – God knows what she must think of me.'

He swept his hand through his springy hair.

'I must go to her. I must go now.'

'Wait until the morning, Jim,' Anthony said as Jim made as if to leave that very moment.

'Of course,' he sank back into his chair. 'She'll be asleep by the time I reach the city. What time's the first train?'

'Early, very early – about four, I think.'

'I'll be on it,' was Jim's only reply.

Chapter Six

The August morning was strangely dank and cold when Katharine awoke to face yet another day the same as the last. Her restricted view from the window of the street was dull, with little to interest an active mind. If it had not been for the writing of her medical articles, she undoubtedly would have been cast into utter despair. But her common sense still reigned supreme even though she had lost much of her natural gaiety. It was difficult to be bright and smiling when the days were lonely and full of frustration. It would take a saint, and Katharine knew herself to be unworthy of any halo.

The difficulty of dressing herself and preparing her breakfast took some time so that she rose early to be finished her meal by the time her landlady came to wash the dishes for her. The woman was a coarse individual. She coughed and wheezed her way about the house, complaining miserably the whole time.

The doorbell clanged as the woman finished the washing-up.

'Now, 'oo can that be this early?'

She shuffled away. Katharine heard muted voices in the hall and was surprised to hear the woman return to her door.

'You'm got a visitor, Miss Harvey, a gentleman.'

'Come in, Anthony. I thought you were leaving last . . .'

She stopped in amazement, the words dying on her lips as Jim's huge frame filled the doorway. Dimly she heard the landlady's mutterings as she closed the door. But Katharine's eyes were fixed upon Jim's face.

'Katharine.'

'Jim.'

They spoke simultaneously. And then with swift strides Jim was by her side, taking her thin hands in his. He dropped to one knee beside her chair.

'My dear Katharine. What have we done to you? Why didn't you write, let me know? Why?'

And he held her hands firmly looking into her eyes. At last she dragged her eyes away from his intent gaze.

'What was the use? You can do nothing.'

'Katharine, how can you say such a thing?'

She shook her head.

'There's *nothing* anyone can do. I wish you hadn't come,' she added distractedly. 'I look such a mess.'

Jim touched her cheek tenderly with the tips of his fingers.

'You've changed, I'll not deny it. But you're still my Katharine.'

He stood again from where he had crouched beside her. Suddenly he grinned.

'Now, Dr. Harvey, you've no argument this time. You're coming back to Brackenbeck.'

'I can't be a burden on others, Jim. I'd have nowhere to live. I–'

A frown crossed his forehead.

'Are you wilfully misunderstanding me? I mean you to come back as Mrs. Kendrick. And,' as she opened her mouth to protest. 'I won't take 'no' for an answer, this time.'

Katharine's objection was silenced by his lips. But not for long.

'Jim, Jim,' she gasped, breaking free. 'I can't. How can I marry you now? After refusing you in favour of my career, do you think I could be so cruel as to make you take second best? I have been prevented from practising by misfortune. Do you think I could inflict my suffering on you, besides being a burden to you?'

'But it's because of me you're crippled.'

Katharine searched his face.

'And is that why you're asking me to marry you now? Because you're sorry for me and feel responsible.'

'Katharine!' He moved back as if she had struck him. 'How can you say such a thing when you know how much – how deeply I love you?'

'I'm sorry – I'm sorry. I hardly know what I'm saying. Don't you see, it would be so unfair of me? What would everyone think?'

'I'm not concerned with others. All I want to know, need to know, is – do you care for me at all?'

He knelt beside her chair again. She lifted her face slowly to look at him, the tears coursing down her cheeks. She touched his bronzed face with her fingers. There was a long pause before she spoke. Slowly she shook her head.

'I don't know. I just don't know. When you asked me to marry you that day before I left Brackenbeck, on the hillside, remember?'

Jim nodded.

'Do you think I could have forgotten?' he murmured wryly, for a moment the hurt returning in full measure.

'I told you then,' Katharine continued, 'that if I ever did care for anyone it would be for you.'

'Then . . .'

She silenced him with her fingers on his lips.

'But now, since this has happened to me, I don't *feel* anything. It's as if not only my legs are paralysed by my heart also. I can only remember that when I left you, I missed you more than I had believed it possible. So much that I almost came back – several times.'

'If only you had.'

She shook her head.

'No, when finally I knew this was going to happen, I was glad I had not done so. I hoped you would never hear about it. When Anthony arrived out of the blue the other day I was so glad to see him, to see an old friend and yet so surprised after all this time, and so careful to avoid your name, that it was not until he had gone that I realised I had not begged him to keep my secret.'

'Do you suppose he would have done so, even if you had asked him?'

Katharine looked at him searching his eyes and seeing again his love for her.

'I – he never mentioned you either. I didn't know what to think after he had gone. He never really spoke of Brackenbeck, for all I knew he no longer lived there. Or perhaps you had left.'

She looked down at his clothes, seeing for the first time, the difference in his dress from when she had first known him in Brackenbeck. Gone were the rough workmen's clothes, and in their place, he wore a fashionable double-breasted frock coat with a grey waistcoat of good material and fine cut, and the top hat which he had laid on the table on entry, Katharine now noticed, was of beaver.

'You seem to have prospered,' she murmured, suddenly feeling lost and out of touch, knowing nothing of the happenings to Jim during the past five years.

Jim shrugged.

'My father died a few months after you left. He left me everything, though I divided it between Mary and myself.'

Katharine smiled tentatively, memories flooding back now.

'Mary – and Tom, how are they? Anthony did tell me in one of his letters that Tom did not lose his leg. I was so glad.'

Jim's face sobered. He rose and stood near the window looking out. She sensed he was seeing not the street but the scene of five years ago, the accident, the tunnel, Tom's wound and Katharine.

Katharine's words broke into his thoughts.

'Little Tommy? How is he?'

'He's fine, a growing boy. Of course, you don't know about little Kate?'

'Kate?' Katharine whispered.

'Yes, they had a little girl, she's three now. She just about lives with me.'

He looked down at Katharine.

'They called her after you, my dear,' he said gently.

Katharine did not answer.

'I've had a long time to think since you left Brackenbeck,' Jim said quietly. 'I've learnt to see that you did what you thought was right, your duty, even though it cost happiness, mine certainly, and possibly your own too. But don't you see, for better or worse, we've been given a second chance? You've no obligation to the medical profession now.'

Katharine's eyes darkened.

'No. They have turned away from me when I needed them most. Oh, I don't mean they haven't been kindness itself, and everything has been done in the way of treatment, but I think I could have stayed on in an advisory capacity even if I could not practice fully. I could have done something, anything but this useless existence.'

'Could you, Kate? Be honest, could you really?'

'H-how do you mean?'

She looked up at him puzzled.

'Never mind,' he murmured. 'Let's think no more about the past. Let's plan for the future – our future.'

'No, Jim, no. I cannot, I should not, marry you.'

'Do you really not want to, my dear?'

'No, yes, no, I don't know what I *do* want,' she said distractedly.

'Listen,' he said gently. 'You're ill now, low and dispirited. When we get back to Brackenbeck, in the good Yorkshire air, you'll soon be fit and well and then, I hope you'll return my love.'

She looked up at him. He was so tall and strong, so fine-looking in his smart town clothes. She certainly felt an overwhelming sense of gratitude for his continued love for her after all that had happened.

But was she merely seeking release from the prison of her lonely room?

'You're coming to Brackenbeck and as my wife,' Jim said firmly.

Her further arguments, half-hearted as they were, were futile against his resolve and finally she gave way. She had neither the strength of will nor the desire to fight him any longer. She had hurt him enough in the past. When he had offered her love and security, she had spurned him in favour of her career – that fickle, inanimate object, which, in turn, she felt had rejected her because of her physical disability. She felt, rather than knew, that it was because she was a woman and the majority feeling was that she would not be sorely missed. Had an eminent surgeon or a brilliant consultant been so struck down, she felt that heaven and earth would have been moved to try and find some way to keep him in practice.

But Jim had come back to her when she most needed him. Katharine could not, though she felt she were giving him only second best, reject him again, even though all feeling in her seemed to have gone. At this time she did not care whether she married Jim and returned to Brackenbeck or stayed alone in this dingy room.

In short, life had no meaning for her.

She tried, however, to let none of this feeling transmit itself to Jim, but though he never said anything to her, she sometimes caught him looking at her with deep concern in his eyes, mingled with hurt and fear.

At these times she would feel ashamed when he was giving her so much and she giving him so little in return.

Katharine was surprised at the speed with which Jim put his plans into action. He arranged for them to be married in a small church in London by special licence, though how he managed it she did not know. She knew he would have much preferred to have been married in his birthplace, Brackenbeck, but here again, Katharine realised, he was considering her feelings, knowing instinctively without asking her that she would not wish to be the centre of attention – in her invalid chair.

Elizabeth, her friend from the hospital, the sister whom the matron had spoken of to Anthony, came one afternoon when Katharine was alone. She related to Elizabeth the happenings of the past day or two and asked for help.

'Of course, Katharine. Oh, I'm so happy for you. So glad you're going to get out of this place. He must be a wonderful man, your Jim.'

'He is, he is,' Katharine replied and knew she meant it. 'You'll meet him later, but I want you to buy a dress for me. A white one, something suitable for – this,' she indicated her bathchair with hatred.

'You leave it to Aunty Elizabeth. When is the service? May I come?'

'Would you?' Katharine said with gratitude. 'Oh, that would be lovely.'

'Try and keep me away,' Elizabeth laughed.

When Elizabeth returned to Katharine a little over two hours later, Jim had returned. As he took the huge box from Elizabeth's arms, Katharine introduced them.

'I'm very pleased to meet you, Mr. Kendrick.'

'And I you, Miss – er . . .'

'Please call me Elizabeth.'

'And please call me Jim.'

They laughed together.

'Katharine tells me how good you have been to her, Elizabeth. I must thank you.'

'It's nothing, I wish I could have done more.'

Katharine saw them both turn to look at her and she turned her eyes away.

'Come, show me the dress,' she said to Elizabeth.

'Not whilst Jim is here, it's unlucky.'

Jim laughed.

'It's time I was going anyway. There are one or two other things I still have to do.'

He bent to kiss Katharine.

'Goodbye, my love.'

And, after a further exchange of conversation with Elizabeth regarding arrangements for the morrow, Jim left.

'He's nice,' Elizabeth said simply as the door closed behind him. 'How lucky you are.'

Katharine did not reply. In her invalid's chair, she felt far from lucky.

The dress, though not a wedding dress but a theatre gown, was of white tulle on taffeta with fine needlepoint-lace embroidery. The blouse bodice was high-necked, with sleeves to the elbow.

'I bought this lace hat too with this pretty ostrich plume,' Elizabeth said, 'and gloves, of course. Oh, and shoes – will these fit?'

Katharine put them on her tiny feet.

'Perfect, Elizabeth. However did you manage it?'

'Come, try the dress on, Katharine, for if it is the wrong fit I have only tomorrow morning in which to change it if you're to be married at two o'clock.'

Because of Katharine's disability, they had some difficulty, but at last she was arrayed in the dress. It fitted perfectly and Katharine had never possessed a prettier one.

'It's – lovely,' she said.

'You don't sound very enthusiastic,' Elizabeth said softly and a little sadly. Thinking she had hurt Elizabeth's feelings by insinuating that she did not like the dress, Katharine tried to reassure her friend.

'The dress is beautiful, but – but how can I hope to do it justice like this?'

Elizabeth sighed and then she laughed.

'Katharine, you are indulging in self-pity again. You've no need now, you know. Snap out of it.'

Katharine smiled wryly at her friend's attempts to help her.

'I'm unworthy of anyone's trouble, I . . .'

'Katharine Harvey – stop it. I shall get angry. There's that nice man going to marry you and look after you for the rest of your life, and it will be for life, let me tell you. He's no man to go back on his word, I can tell in a minute . . .'

'But . . .'

'But nothing. He adores you, anyone can see that,' she sighed. 'I'm really quite envious of you, I wish I had a man to love me like that.'

Katharine was silent. She felt ashamed. Elizabeth was right. And yet, she herself was right also, she was unworthy of anyone's trouble, and of Jim's love.

'Now,' Elizabeth said briskly. 'I'm going to wash your hair for you. I'll have you looking a radiant bride if it's the last thing I do.'

And when half past one the following afternoon arrived, Katharine looked, if not exactly radiant, at least prettier and a little happier than when Jim had seen her for the first time after five years. But she was still a shadow of the spirited girl she had been on her first arrival in Brackenbeck and she knew it. She sat before her mirror on her wedding morning and looked long and hard at herself. She saw the hollowness of her cheeks, the large dark eyes, the auburn hair which had lost its healthy, cared-for lustre, in spite of Elizabeth's efforts. Involuntarily, a groan escaped her.

'What can Jim see in me now?' she asked aloud to the empty room. 'He's going to regret today, I know it.'

Katharine had hoped Elizabeth would come in time not only to help her dress but also to reassure her. But her friend must have been delayed at the hospital and Katharine had had to get ready alone. She had hoped too that Elizabeth would be here to take her to the church for she did not know how she was to get there otherwise and she had not thought to ask Jim.

There was a knock at the door.

'Come in, Elizabeth, I thought you were never coming, I'm nearly ready . . .'

But the door opened and Jim stood there. Tall and handsome in his dark suit, completely at ease in such finery, he smiled at her.

'Good morning, Mrs. Kendrick-to-be.'

'Jim, you shouldn't be here. It's unlucky to meet before the wedding. I wish you hadn't come.'

He came in and shut the door.

'I didn't know a level-headed young woman like you was superstitious,' he laughed. 'How did you think you were going to get to the church if I didn't fetch you?'

'I – I don't know. I thought Elizabeth would come, I suppose.'

'Elizabeth has to work until the very last minute, unfortunately, or she would have come. She told you that yesterday.'

'Did she? I can't have been listening.'

Jim shook his head slowly, a slight frown appearing.

'Katharine, you don't seem to be taking a great deal of interest in our wedding. You've left all the plans to me, made no suggestions nor even asked what I've done. Am I really making you marry me against your will?'

Katharine shook her head and twisted her fingers together nervously.

'No, no – of course not,' her voice sounded shrill, totally unlike her own soft tones.

Jim sighed, but said no more but instead handed her a small box.

'I'm afraid we haven't had a proper engagement – but I do so want you to have a ring.'

Opening the box she found, nestling against a black velvet cushion, a ring – three rubies separated by two diamonds. 'With – all my love,' his voice dropped a tone lower on the last three words.

'Jim – it's beautiful. Thank you.'

'Come, it's time we went or the vicar will become impatient,' Jim said. 'Elizabeth will be waiting for us at the church I expect with Dr. Porter.'

He manoeuvred her bathchair from the room and down the steps out of the house. Katharine could not fail to marvel at the ease with which Jim pushed her, and at the gentle care he showed when moving down the steps. Whenever Elizabeth had taken her out, Katharine had dreaded the steps at the front of this house because of the jolting she suffered as the chair bumped down each one. But Jim's strength and his protective care prevented this and she hardly noticed the descent. They moved down the road, Katharine grasping the long stick-like handle to steer the chair.

It was quite a long walk to the church but fortunately the day was fine and warm.

Outside the church, squatting on the steps, was an old woman selling flowers. She crouched there, hugging a tattered shawl about her thin shoulders, a floppy hat covering wispy grey hair and her sunken mouth working in sucking movements.

Against the grey pavement and the dark, rather austere, outline of the church, the small bunches of roses, red, yellow and white, added gaiety and awoke, momentarily, in Katharine an instinctive response.

Impulsively, she caught Jim's arm. 'Jim, I've no flowers. Please buy me some of those beautiful roses.'

She looked up at him and saw the look in his eyes, saw the hope leap there, the hope that she was beginning to take a heartfelt interest in the day's proceedings.

Willingly he stepped forward and, bending down, he spoke to the wizened old woman. Katharine saw her motion towards the basket with a claw-like hand. Jim's strong hands reached down and gathered several bunches together – all red roses. Lifting them out gently, he carried them back to Katharine and placed them in her lap to make a splash of vivid colour against her white dress. She saw the smile on his face, and, as she turned, she saw a slow smile of realisation spread across the toothless mouth of the old flower-seller.

'Gawd bless you, ducks,' the old woman croaked as Jim placed several silver coins in her bony hand.

The progress up the numerous steps and into the porchway of the church was slow. But Jim, so strong and patient, was not even breathing heavily when they reached the top. Elizabeth and Dr. Porter, who had agreed at Elizabeth's request to give the bride away awaited them in the porch. Elizabeth smiled her welcome and squeezed Katharine's hand and Dr. Porter shook hands with Jim and smiled benignly down at Katharine, his white moustache quivering.

The muted tones of the organ drifted from the dim interior and as Jim opened the heavy door and wheeled Katharine into the church, she smelt the polish of the pews, the mustiness of old prayer books and the scent of flowers, dying now since the previous Sunday.

The vicar moved forward to meet them. As they reached the steps, he stooped down and took Katharine's hands in his.

'My dear child,' was all he said, but Katharine could read the meaning in his kindly tone. She glanced up at her groom. Tall and proud he stood beside her, his hand still on the back of her chair, protectively.

She looked towards the altar and saw the small ivory carving of Christ on the cross. It was exquisite and, if she half-closed her eyes, almost life-like, though so small.

I should be making thanks with all my heart for my good fortune in the love of this man, she thought, suddenly filled with guilt. And yet, still she could feel nothing. Her heart was cold as stone.

The service began, the vicar reading the solemn words carefully and lovingly. Jim, clasping her hand, made his response firmly, his bass tone ringing through the empty church. On the other side of her stood Dr. Porter with Elizabeth behind them. Dr. Porter had been the doctor with whom Katharine had worked closely and whom she had been assisting when she had collapsed. Though she owed him a great deal for his kindness, Katharine still could not help but envy him, for he was still practising medicine and she . . .

'Repeat after me,' the vicar was saying. Katharine brought her wandering thoughts back to the present. She made her responses in low, flat tones, wishing with every word that she could put more feeling into her voice. But she had never been any good at acting, at pretending something she did not, and could not, feel.

The vicar had taken care of all the formalities as regards witnesses and his sympathetic handling of the occasion would long be remembered by Katharine with gratitude. She felt nothing in the way of acute embarrassment, as she had feared, as a bathchair bride. Soon they were leaving the church. The vicar followed them to the door wishing them happiness and pressing them to come and see him again should they ever be in the vicinity.

'And you must come and visit us at Brackenbeck, if you ever come to Yorkshire. You would be most welcome,' said Jim.

'I might at that, young man,' said the elderly man, nodding his silvery head. 'My parents came from Yorkshire. I may well take advantage of your invitation.'

As they came down the church steps again, Katharine noticed the flower-seller was no longer there.

'I'm sorry, but I must leave you now,' Dr. Porter was saying. And he shook Jim's hand again. 'Good luck to you both and come and see us again. Goodbye, Dr. Harvey, it's been a pleasure to know you.'

'Goodbye,' Katharine said quietly.

'Thank you for coming, Dr. Porter,' Jim put in courteously.

So it was over, Katharine mused. This was goodbye to London, to the hospital, to the medical profession.

'And I must dash too,' Elizabeth interrupted her thoughts. 'I'm on duty again in half-an-hour, I had to get special permission to come.'

'Elizabeth, don't . . .' Katharine was about to say 'don't go', but realising swiftly how it would seem to those about her, especially to Jim, she altered her words quickly. 'Don't forget to write and to come and see us soon, very soon.'

'Yes, please do, Elizabeth,' Jim added.

Elizabeth smiled at them.

'I should love to come. I've never been to Yorkshire.'

'Then you *must* come,' laughed Jim in mock scandalised tones.

Elizabeth laughed too, but Katharine found it an effort to smile.

Then, with further promises and good wishes, Elizabeth left them.

'Shall we walk back again, Katharine?' Jim asked. 'It's not far. Will you be warm enough?'

'Yes, of course. But I hate being pushed along the street. It's so humiliating.'

'But Katharine, my love, you must accept it. How are we to get about at home?'

'I shan't want to get about. I shall be quite content to stay at home.'

'Well, I shan't.'

'Then you must go out on your own.'

'Katharine, I love the countryside around Brackenbeck. The moors, the becks and hills. I want to share them with you. Don't you understand? I don't want to go out on my own any more, I don't want to be alone and lonely any longer.'

Katharine was silent.

'We'll go and collect your things and then go on to the hotel,' Jim said.

'The hotel?'

'Why, yes. I've booked a room for us there.'

'No, Jim. I'd rather stay at my lodgings.'

'But I can't stay ...' He stopped and then added, 'Why don't you want to come to the hotel, Katharine?'

'Jim, I shall feel so awkward at such a place in this dreadful chair. Please, try to understand. Please, let me stay at my lodgings – just tonight?'

Jim sighed.

'Very well, my dear.'

And so Katharine spent one more night in her dismal room and Jim returned to his hotel. The first night of their marriage they spent two miles apart.

The next morning Katharine had only just finished dressing when Jim arrived.

'Good morning, Mrs. Kendrick,' he teased and even raised a smile from her.

Jim saw the landlady and paid the rent Katharine owed, whilst she sat in her chair feeling useless and helpless. Jim was cheerful, but rather quiet, saying little after his first gay greeting. She could not read his expression nor guess his thoughts. Was he, even now, she wondered, realising what a task he had undertaken?

The journey to Yorkshire was long and tedious, made more so by Katharine's awkwardness. She felt a burden to Jim. If she felt this now, on the first day as his wife, what could she expect to feel in the years ahead? She should have spoken out against Jim, she told herself, against their marriage before it was too late.

But she voiced none of these misgivings to her husband. She sat, instead, huddled in her chair on the draughty stations where they had to change trains, or leaning back in the carriage gazing out at the flashing scenery, silent and remote. Jim, too, seemed occupied with his own thoughts and this made Katharine all the more depressed.

Their arrival at the station near Brackenbeck was unheralded and therefore unexpected. There was no welcome, no pony and trap. Not even Jim's famous motor car, for no doubt no one but he knew how to drive it, or, for that matter, dare to do so.

This meant a long, tiring walk for Jim.

'Can you not find a trap, Jim?' Katharine asked, raising herself from her thoughts.

'I shall enjoy it, Katharine my love. You'll not be cold though?'

'No, only it's such a long way, all of four miles and pushing me up the hills and . . .'

'You're as light as a feather, lass.'

She looked up at him. 'You said that to me once before.'

'Ay, I remember. Katharine, it's grand to be back home and with you here,' he added impulsively, bending down in front of her. 'Say you're glad to be here.'

'I am glad – but I'm frightened.'

'Frightened? Whatever for?'

She shrugged and fingered the rug which wrapped her legs warmly.

'Oh, of meeting everyone again and – and them seeing me like this.'

'And how do you think they're going to feel when they remember why you *are* like this?'

Katharine looked up sharply.

'I don't want pity, not from them or – or you.'

'Katharine, Katharine, be generous. People give you pity only when they care about you. So many people shy from receiving pity but sincere pity is given mingled with love. Don't try to shut everyone from your life, my love. Let people help you when they want to.'

Again she felt ashamed and yet there was still the nagging doubt that Jim had married her out of pity and a sense of guilt.

They said no more, but started off over the moors. It seemed a long road, far longer than when she had travelled it herself on foot on her visit to Brackenbeck, and again when leaving, every step taking her away from the valley and away from Jim.

And now, five years later, she was returning, with Jim as her husband. But her return was not in the style she would have wished.

Grey clouds scudded across the sky and a sharp breeze whipped across the moors reminding her of the bleakness of this part of the world.

But to Jim this was home. This was where he belonged.

'We haven't time to linger today, Katharine, but there's so much hidden beauty on these moors. See over there?'

Jim pointed and Katharine followed the line of his finger.

'The top of that sycamore?'

'Yes, I see.'

'Do you see it's the only one around here? It's too bleak for many trees, but that tree grows from a steep little dell where there's a spring of running water. It's shady too. Almost like an oasis in a desert.'

'Yes, yes,' Katharine said, willing herself to interest and enthusiasm. 'Those trees up there on the skyline, they look so stark, somehow.'

'They have a job to survive or grow at all in the weather we get up on these moors.'

Katharine shivered.

'Are you cold, my dear?'

'No – no, not really. But it's so lonely up here. So bleak and cold.'

Jim laughed.

'I love these moors, I always have done. And I never found them lonely until . . .' his tone sobered, 'until you left, Katharine. Since then, these last five years, I've found them very lonely. But then, I would have been lonely anywhere.'

Then as they capped the hill leading down into the dale of Brackenbeck all the memories of her previous visit came flooding back to her.

And as they neared Kendrick House.

'Jim, what a difference you've made to the road to Kendrick House.'

She was remembering the neglected, overgrown pathway, which had now been cleared and a proper road led up to the gate.

Here, the moss had been removed from the wall and the nameplate was clearly visible. The wrought-iron gates were no longer rusty but painted black and as Jim pushed her chair through, she saw the gardens were neat and cared-for. The house too had been painted and lights shone from every downstairs window for it was already dusk.

Now the house seemed to say to her 'Look, here I am, look how different I am now someone cares for me'.

The front door opened and a woman came running down the steps to meet them.

'Mr. Kendrick, you've brought her back to us, sir.'

'Yes, Mrs. Johnson. Katharine, you remember Mrs. Johnson? She's my housekeeper now.'

'Of course,' and Katharine held out her hand to the woman who bobbed an embarrassed curtsy. It had been Mrs. Johnson who had comforted Mary at the quarry on the day of the accident, Katharine recalled.

'Mrs. Johnson,' Jim was saying, 'you shall be the first to know. This is Mrs. Kendrick.'

Katharine watched the woman's reactions carefully. Mrs. Johnson's surprise was genuine and the smile faded a little as her mouth dropped open. She glanced swiftly at the invalid chair and back again to Jim's smiling face. Katharine saw the visible change in the woman's expression. As if reading the happiness in Jim's face – a look she had rarely seen and never of late, Katharine guessed – Mrs. Johnson broke into ecstasies of delight, clapping her hands and 'oh'ing and 'ah'ing.

'Oh, come in, madam, oh dear, I'm reet flustered. Dear, dear, what surprises tha does spring on us, Mr. Kendrick. Well, I never did!'

The rotund form of the bustling Mrs. Johnson preceded them up the steps and she turned to watch at the top as Jim turned the chair round and carefully manoeuvred it up the steps. Katharine felt a rush of embarrassment and knew how often she would have to face the same feeling.

'Come in, come in, I've got a good fire going in the drawing-room, sir.'

'Thank you, Mrs. Johnson.'

'Is there anything else I can do, ma'am?'

'No – no, thank you, Mrs. Johnson,' Katharine faltered. She was unused to servants for although her parents had had a maid, it was so long ago, and so much seemed to have happened since that time that Katharine had forgotten.

'Dinner will be a little late, sir, about an hour.'

'That'll be all right, Mrs. Johnson.'

'How many servants have you got, Jim?' Katharine asked when Mrs. Johnson had left the room.

'Mrs. Johnson as housekeeper, cook – that's Mrs. Manners. Arthur, the man-servant-cum-butler, and Lucy, the maid,' replied Jim.

'Good gracious! I never imagined you as having servants at all, let alone so many.'

Jim laughed.

'Times have changed since you were here.'

'They certainly have.'

'Mrs. Johnson and a girl from the village used to come in daily at the cottage, but no one lived in. Mrs. Johnson's husband was Simon Johnson, the man who owned Brackenbeck quarry before me. I bought it from her when he died. I think things were still a bit hard for her, besides being lonely. So when I offered her a permanent post and a home here, she jumped at the chance.'

'I expect she's not very pleased to see me arrive as mistress of the house. I shall usurp her position.'

Jim chuckled.

'Mrs. Johnson hardly enjoyed the same position as you, my love.'

And Katharine smiled slightly.

'I've been thinking,' Jim said, 'although it's rather late, I think I ought to fetch Anthony to have dinner with us. Would you mind, Katharine? After all, he should learn our news from us, and if I know my staff, somehow the news will be all round the village before nightfall. I think we owe it to him, seeing as he brought us together again.'

Katharine thought fleetingly of Anthony's vague proposal and wondered whether he would be pleased or sorry at their news.

'Of course,' was all she replied to her husband.

Jim disappeared down the drive in his motor car, Katharine watching its progress with a half-hearted interest. The machine was certainly something out of the ordinary.

She had to remain where Jim had left her, sitting in a wing armchair between the fire and the long drawing-room window, which faced out over the valley of Brackenbeck. He had positioned the chair with thought, so that she not only felt the warmth of the fire, but could also take full advantage of the view from the window.

Katharine, left alone, looked about her. The room was long and narrow. The carpet and furniture were fairly new, having been bought, she supposed, when Jim took up residence here. The overall colour scheme was royal blue, with curtains and upholstery matching. The effect was neither pretentious nor too-luxurious, but comfortable and well-planned. Katharine wondered how much had been Jim's personal choice and how much Mrs. Johnson's hand.

She wished she could get to her bedroom and freshen up before dinner, but short of asking Mrs. Johnson there was no means of doing so until Jim returned. And then Anthony would be with him.

But at that moment Mrs. Johnson returned.

'Madam, I was wondering, that is, were you awanting to go upstairs?'

The woman was obviously ill-at-ease, and Katharine forgot her own embarrassment in trying to eradicate Mrs. Johnson's.

'I would rather like to go to my room, but you cannot possibly carry me upstairs – I'm afraid that is the only way I could get there. I wouldn't dream of letting you try.'

'But Arthur could, ma'am. If you'd let him, that is.'

Katharine hesitated. Then she took a deep breath. She would have to accept help from others. Jim would not always be available to move her about.

'Very well, Mrs. Johnson,' she said resignedly.

The journey upstairs was accomplished with patient care by Arthur, a middle-aged man with a pleasant, impassive face, and, much to Katharine's surprise, with comfort. It seemed she was no great burden to him.

'Thank you, Arthur,' she was able to say warmly when they reached the bedroom and he set her carefully in a chair at the dressing-table. Arthur inclined his head slightly in a respectful bow but said nothing, although she read the sympathy, kindly meant, in his eyes.

This was the principal bedroom, light and airy.

'Er, I don't rightly know how to say this, madam, and begging your pardon, but . . .'

'Yes, Mrs. Johnson.'

'Well, Mr. Kendrick hasn't employed a personal maid for you as yet, and in the meantime, if there's anything I can do for you, madam, well, you've only got to say.'

Katharine smiled and much of her embarrassment slipped away. The woman was obviously trying to offer her help and yet felt awkward at doing so, not wishing to give offence. Jim had been right. People did genuinely want to help her.

'I can see you're going to be a great ally, Mrs. Johnson. And I regret to have to say that I shall probably often need your help,' Katharine added ruefully.

'Well, don't tha be shy to say whenever tha wants me, ma'am.'

Mrs. Johnson was obviously the motherly type, but for this Katharine was grateful. She could not help but compare the difference between Mrs. Johnson and Mrs. Rigby. She shuddered to think that it might have been the latter here instead of this kindly person.

By the time Jim and Anthony returned, Katharine had not only freshened up her travel-stained appearance, but had also, with both Arthur's and Mrs. Johnson's help, been on a fully conducted tour of the house, and was once more installed in the drawing-room.

'Well, well, well,' Anthony came in rubbing his hands. 'Good to see you again, Kate. Back where you belong. Where are you staying?'

Jim came in behind him.

'That's what we want to tell you, Anthony. We were married yesterday.'

Anthony sat down suddenly. His face gave away the fact that although he had half-expected it, having been instrumental in reuniting them, nevertheless, the suddenness was still a shock.

'My congratulations,' he said, shaking hands with Jim and at the same time searching Katharine's eyes as if to read her deepest feelings. She avoided his questioning gaze.

Throughout dinner the two men kept up the flow of conversation for which Katharine was thankful. She was tired after the journey and neither was she ready to make light conversation nor to answer questions about her life during the past five years. But at the end of the meal Anthony said,

'I suppose I shouldn't have been surprised to hear of your marriage, after all, I sent you to her didn't I? But . . .'

He stopped, as if in embarrassment.

'You thought he wouldn't ask me now,' said Katharine in her curiously flat voice.

'No, no,' said Anthony quickly. 'I knew Jim would *ask* – but I thought you would not accept – more than ever now, knowing you.'

Before she could reply, Jim said,

'I bullied her into it, wouldn't take no this time. I think she's still in a dazed state of shock,' he teased, smiling. 'Can you prescribe anything, doctor?'

Anthony looked at her soberly.

'You've changed, Kate, but I hope you'll become what you were before, when you've been with us a while.'

Katharine looked away unable to speak. She knew herself, without being told, that she was suffering from deep melancholia – she was not a doctor for nothing.

But at the present time the physician could not heal herself.

'Well, I must be going,' Anthony said.

'Come and see us any time, Anthony, you know you're always welcome,' Jim said.

'Thanks, and I'll see what I can do to help.'

He leant down and rested his hands on the arms of her chair, looking directly into her eyes.

'You need help, don't you, Katharine?'

After a moment she nodded dully.

'If only I could walk again,' she whispered, but knew that both men heard her.

'Perhaps you will, perhaps it's not so hopeless as they made out, Kate,' Anthony said.

But Jim's voice cut in sharply.

'No. I mean – she's no need to do more damage to herself – by – forcing herself to try and walk. I'll look after her. She's no need to walk.'

Katharine stared at him, startled by the vehemence in his tone. The deep frown had returned to his face and the haunted look to his eyes. It was exactly the same expression she had seen darken his face when she had left him five years before.

After Jim's outburst, Anthony's leavetaking was slightly strained. Naturally, from a doctor's point of view, Anthony's goal was a cure for her, whilst, it now appeared that Jim was quite content to let her remain tied to her bathchair.

Katharine was shocked by this unexpected revelation of Jim's feeling and not a little hurt by it.

Why, she asked herself, should he want me to stay like this?

And although the matter was not referred to again between Jim and Katharine, the incident had left her wondering.

Chapter Seven

The first full day after their arrival back in Brackenbeck was taken up almost entirely with callers at Kendrick House. The first of these, and, from Katharine's point of view, the most welcome, were the Gifford family. As soon as they entered the house Katharine could hear the excited chatter of the children and the quiet tones of Mary trying to quieten her lively offspring. Tom came in first, his grin stretching from ear to ear, and without a glance at the bathchair, he clasped her hands warmly, but not before Katharine's professional interest had noted that his injured leg was stiff and that it still caused him to limp.

'Reet glad we are to see thee back, lass.'

The children sidled in, pushed by their mother, shy now that they were to meet their new aunt. The little girl, Katharine, spotted her favourite person.

'Uncle Jim, Uncle Jim,' and her round little arms stretched out to Jim and she trotted towards him with a cherubic beam. Jim swung the small girl high above his head and perched her upon his broad shoulder, whilst the child gurgled happily. There were certainly none of the restrictions imposed upon these children by which most children were ruled.

Little Tommy, now a sturdy boy of seven, was not to be left out of his uncle's attentions and noisily clamoured to be lifted on to his other shoulder.

'Children, children, what will your Aunt Katharine think of you?' remonstrated Mary in her soft voice.

But the children merely beamed delightedly at their aunt and then turned their attention back to their uncle. Katharine watched them, feeling, for the moment, left out of their family. Could they ever really accept her as one of themselves? But Mary's welcome was warmth itself. Her pleasure was genuine, Katharine was sure. And she gave no indication that she disapproved of her crippled sister-in-law. Perhaps, Katharine though she had had some notion that this was what Jim had in mind when he had left for London and consequently the news was no great surprise to her.

As Katherine watched Jim with his nephew and niece, it became apparent to her that he adored children. There was nothing, she supposed, to prevent her having children, but if not impossible, it would certainly be difficult.

She sighed to herself. There were going to be many things which were difficult, she could see that.

The days slid by forming a pattern. Jim stayed with her as much as possible, but he was obliged, at times, to visit his various farmlands and even the quarries, where he was often needed to give Tom advice. He tried frequently to persuade Katharine to go with him.

'You would be quite comfortable in the motor car, Katharine. It would do you good to come out.'

But Katharine would shake her head and avoid his eyes. She clung to the safe confines of Kendrick House. She went out into the garden, either with Jim's help or with Arthur – but no further.

It was from Arthur that she learnt more about Jim's family, for she hesitated to broach the subject with her husband and yet she was curious. As Arthur pushed her chair round the garden one comparatively warm autumn afternoon, Katharine said,

'Arthur, Mr. Kendrick tells me that you were with his father for a number of years. Tell me, what was he like?'

Arthur cleared his throat self-consciously.

'I don't think it my place, ma'am, to give my opinions on Mr. Kendrick's family.'

'Oh please, Arthur. I promise you this conversation will go no further. I shall not take offence at anything you say, and I certainly shall not repeat it, least of all to my husband.'

There was a moment's pause before Arthur said softly. 'There were never two more different people, ma'am, than Mr. Kendrick and master Jim. I first went into Mr. Kendrick's employ when master Jim was twelve years old, and Mary a pretty little lass of four. They were sweet children, ma'am, but sad. They had everything material anyone could wish for, the parents were quite well off then. But they lacked affection. Little Mary clung to her brother and he to her. Two years after I went there, ma'am, Mrs. Kendrick took off and we never saw her again. They was always rowing, you know. I've seen them poor children sat on the stairs, Mary clinging to her brother, weeping, and him, master Jim, with his face set and his eyes dark with anger, and that at twelve or thirteen. Just the time when a lad should be carefree and happy.

'Things were a bit easier, I think, after she went, but their father took to drink. Jim was sent away to school eventually and Mary lived with an aunt for some time. When Jim left school and came home at about eighteen, everyone thought he'd go into farming wi' his father, anyway, seems the cussed old devil, begging your pardon, ma'am, but it's no more than he deserves.'

'It's all right, Arthur, do go on.'

'Well, ma'am, Mr. Kendrick and master Jim had a blazing row, no one knew what about, but off went master Jim to live on his own. And him not a penny to 'is name, mark you.'

'Where was Mary then?' Katharine asked.

'She was still with her aunt, a sister of Mr. Kendrick's, severe and strait-laced as they come. Poor little girl got no affection from that sour faced old bird either.'

Katharine could not resist a smile but was pleased that Arthur, pushing her chair, could not see her smiling at his tirade against her husband's family.

'Anyway, master Jim was not one to be beaten. He worked for Mr. Johnson at the quarry. He started work for him when he was eighteen, and seven years later, old Johnson died and Jim bought the quarry. In the meantime Mary had come to live with Jim in his little cottage and had met Tom Gifford. They wanted to be married but as she was under age, they had to get the old man's permission. They had another big quarrel, old Kendrick and Mary this time. Although she's a quiet little thing, ma'am, she's got a will of iron if she really wants something, and she wanted to marry Tom Gifford all right. Well, in the end the old man gave his consent, but more or less disowned her. Left her none of his money in his will, but, of course, master Jim put that right and Mary's well taken care of now.'

'How did old Mr. Kendrick come to own the other three quarries?'

'The old devil bought them as soon as he heard Jim had bought the Brackenbeck quarry, just so his son couldn't buy them and get on. It's a wonder, really, that he left his money to Jim, when all's done and said, but they seemed to patch up their quarrel just before the old man died.'

'And Jim's mother, what of her?'

'We heard she died about two years ago. Jim and Mary never saw her again from when she left them years before.'

'How terrible!'

'It is, ma'am, but they're both all right now. Mary's happy as can be, and so's master Jim – now, ma'am, if you don't mind me saying so.'

Katharine didn't mind him saying so and yet, she felt guilty. I must try to pull myself together and regain my old cheerfulness, she told herself sternly, but she knew that she could never recapture her full measure of vivacity unless she could walk again.

The days grew into weeks, each a replica of the last. The monotony would normally have driven Katharine, the old Katharine, to distraction, but now she lived in a kind of apathetic stupor.

Christmas was fast approaching and Katharine found, against her will almost, that she was drawn into the festivities. Cook and Mrs. Johnson were constantly asking for her orders and advice as regards their preparations, so much so that Katharine began to wonder if there were not an ulterior motive in their persistence.

It was as if they were trying to force her, however gently and unobtrusively, to take an interest. Jim too was full of enthusiastic plans for Christmas.

'We'll have Mary, Tom and the children here for the day. And Anthony, too, if he likes. I'll get a big tree for the hall. Oh, and by the way I shall get a little present for each of the village children. Will you think of gifts for them, Katharine my love.'

'I'll try, Jim. But how shall I know what they'd like? I don't know them.'

'Children are all the same. You'll think of something they'll love, I'm sure.'

But Katharine was not so sure. She made half-hearted attempts to make out a list and soon small scraps of paper with half-finished lists of suggested gifts were to be found in all parts of the house. In the end, Mary came to her rescue. It seemed that Jim had bestowed the task upon his sister the previous year and she confided to Katharine that she had experienced much the same difficulty.

Gifts for the family were easily settled between Jim and Katharine, but on her gift for him, she could not decide. Again she sought Mary's guidance.

'Oh, dear, I really don't know. I'll have to think about it, Katharine. I'll ask Tom what he thinks.' She giggled. 'Isn't it fun, all this present buying? But it's a worry when you can't think what to get.'

Katharine tried to smile. For years she had had no one for whom to buy a Christmas gift and now here she was surrounded by a loving husband and his affectionate family and still she could not call forth any enthusiasm. Where usually she felt shame and guilt sweep over her, for the first time she felt angry with herself and vowed that she would not let her misery spoil the Kendrick family's Christmas.

And so it was only through the strength of that resolve that she was able, for once, to put on an act during the festivities. Christmas Day was bleak and cold, but devoid of the snow for which the children had hoped.

After breakfast, whilst they waited for their guests, Jim said,

'Katharine, I want to give you my gift now, before the others arrive.'

And before she could protest he left the room returning seconds later with a huge box. In it she found a beautiful coat, of simple lines, but trimmed with sable.

'I thought it would keep you warm in the motor,' his eyes searching her face hopefully.

'I don't deserve such a gift, I don't deserve . . .' Tears filled her eyes.

'Katharine, my love, I didn't mean to upset you, what is it?'

'Nothing – nothing it's such a lovely coat and you've bought it because you want me to come out with you, don't you?'

Jim nodded.

'So much,' he clasped her hand, 'so much . . .'

At that minute the front door bell pealed, heralding the arrival of the Gifford family and the moment when Katharine felt she was reaching out towards her husband, feeling really close to him for the first time, was lost.

The day passed in noisy gaiety. The children loved every moment and even the adult members of the family were joyously uninhibited – laughing and joking as if they had not a worry in the world.

Katharine too, surrounded by an aura of love and warmth, felt some of the cold bitterness in her heart melt away and her act at last became the truth. She enjoyed that Christmas Day, and was happy for the first time in five years.

But her new found contentment was shortlived. It seemed that her Christmas Day happiness was superficial and therefore soon to wither and die.

For most people the aftermath of Christmas leaves them feeling deflated, the festivity and joviality at an end with only the first harsh winter months of the New Year as a bleak prospect. But for Katharine the dejection was exaggerated and she sank back into the deep melancholia from which she had suffered for so long – if anything, she sank deeper than ever into the black abyss of misery.

It seemed, however, that plans were afoot to try to draw her out of this and Anthony's arrival at Kendrick House, one cold February day, when Jim was out, seemed to confirm this.

'Kate,' he said coming straight to the point as was his habit. 'I want you to give talks to the mothers of Brackenbeck on the care of their children.'

There was a silence in the drawing-room.

'I couldn't, Anthony.'

'Why not?'

'Well, I can't move about and *do* things. Besides, I don't want to.'

'Katharine Kendrick – what in heaven's name has got into you, woman?' Anthony slapped his thigh and rose from the arm chair where he had been sitting and began to pace the room.

'I'll tell you what you need, my girl, a darned good hiding.'

Since Katharine made no reply, he continued.

'You sit there, wallowing in self-pity instead of using your talents and leading a normal life.'

Another silence.

'Kate,' he said softly now, his anger dying. 'What's wrong? In the old days you'd have flown at me, claws at the ready, after that little lecture. Have you lost all interest in life?'

'Of course not,' she said, twisting her idle hands in her lap. 'I'm needed here at home – with Jim, that's all.'

'I see.'

'No, you don't see. I'm finished with medicine.'

'No, Kate, you're not. A doctor has never "finished" with medicine.'

'I'm not a doctor any longer. They didn't want me any more, remember? I'm just Jim's wife.'

'But that's not enough, is it, for someone like you? Jim wouldn't be against you doing this – to help his own people. It needn't interfere with your home life at all.'

'I – couldn't.'

'I think you're using Jim as an excuse because I've talked to him and he has no objections.'

'Then you'd no right to discuss such things with him before telling me.'

'Kate, I need your help. There's a lot of ignorance amongst these women as regards the upbringing of their children. They're either over-anxious or neglectful. You could teach them so much, Kate.'

'What?'

'General hygiene in the home, a basic knowledge of first-aid – simple dressings and such, besides special help with ante-natal care. There's so much being done in other parts of the country now, Kate, with regard to personal hygiene instruction,' continued Anthony, warming to his subject. 'There's been health visitors visiting mothers in their homes for a few years now. We haven't got one here. I'd like you to do that work, Kate.'

'How can I like *this?*'

'You could if you wanted to do it. Nothing would have beaten the old Kate. Don't you see, it would save lives?'

Katharine made no reply.

Anthony sighed and went towards the door. He turned back briefly.

'You've disappointed me, Kate. I thought you had more spirit than this.'

And he left, slamming the door behind him so that the china in the glass cabinet clattered in protest.

Katharine thought about Anthony's proposition a good deal during the next few days. But in the end she still decided that she could not go out amongst the people of Brackenbeck. She could not bear to be pitied and to know that they were pitying Jim for being tied to a crippled wife.

Jim never mentioned Anthony's idea to her, nor she to him. But he was no longer content to let her hide herself away in Kendrick House.

'Katharine, you're coming out with me on Sunday if it's fine and not too cold.'

'No, Jim, I'd rather not, please.'

The frown returned to his eyes.

'Katharine, you're coming.'

She looked up at him and read the determination in his face. She sighed and said no more. Argument was useless and besides she could not be bothered to argue. She hoped for rain, but the afternoon of the following Sunday was fine and as warm as one could expect on a late February day on the moors. Jim carried her out to the car and solicitously wrapped a warm rug round her.

'It's sometimes rather chilly in this contraption up on the moors,' he joked.

This was the first time Katharine had seen the motor car at close quarters. She found herself sitting high up on the front seat. It was comfortable but as Jim had said, a little draughty, but in her new coat, Katharine was warm enough. The only protection was given by the windscreen.

'I thought we'd drive up on the moors rather than through the village,' Jim said, climbing up beside her. Katharine was grateful for his thoughtfulness.

This was also her first ride in a motor car and for the first time since the accident, she found herself captivated by the experience. They chugged along the road, shouting to each other above the noise.

'Jim, it's marvellous. I had no idea.'

'See what you've been missing. You should have come weeks ago.'

Katharine nodded.

Up on the moors it was cold, but still pleasant. Jim stopped the car on the roadside, right at the edge of the moorland.

Katharine could not help but notice and be amused at the change which came over Jim as they sat in the car gazing at the scene. He was usually rather quiet and reserved, even though he was obviously so much happier, but here on the moors it was as if a spring were released in him and all his love for the moorlands and hills was unleashed and came rushing out like the bubbling beck itself. He knew the moorlands in every season, knew their every mood – the bitter cruelty of their savage winter, the unwilling spring and then the summer, never warm, but always retaining that austerity, and still he loved them and never seemed to tire of talking of them or visiting them. His eyes would roam over the dark, craggy hills rising from the moors covered with heather or springy bracken. The long rough grass waved in the breeze and always, not far distant, there seemed to be the sound of rushing water, for everywhere there seemed to be streams tumbling over the rough rocks hurtling down, twisting and gurgling.

The whole effect was of sombre, massive beauty, but Katharine felt it was a man's country, the only delicate beauty seeming to be the white-boiled cotton grass on the moors and the blue harebells. The curlew, with its melancholy cry as if he too mourned the bleakness of the place, wheeled above them. Only the acrobatic lapwing, the bird Katharine had seen on her first arrival, but whose name she only learnt now from Jim, seemed incongruous in the sorrowful, desolate surroundings. Even the grouse with its 'go-back, go-back' cry, seemed to reject visitors to its domain.

The moors and hills were home to Jim and the car rides to the moors became more frequent in the spring and summer. But Katharine hardly enjoyed them, her first interest in his motor having waned, and she would long to return home. All the time she remained silent, listening to Jim, but still taking no really active part, no lively, questioning interest.

At times she would see him watching her, the frown deep on his forehead and his eyes full of untold misery.

And she would feel ashamed.

July brought a letter from Elizabeth.

'I have two weeks' holiday, next month,' she wrote, 'though how I've managed it I don't know. We're so short of staff at the moment. I wonder if I might come north to see you? The coolness of those moors of Jim's are calling me from these sun-baked streets. Oh Katharine, it's unbearably hot here . . .'

Katharine was delighted. At last a contact with her hospital – only it was no longer hers.

But she awaited Elizabeth's arrival with pleasurable anticipation – eager for news of the world she had left behind and for which she still hungered. She voiced none of this to her husband, but, although he too seemed pleased at the prospect of a visit from Elizabeth, she wondered whether the puzzled look so often in his eyes now included surprise at the change in Katharine. She knew herself to be looking forward to her friend's visit and she could not hide it. Her eyes were brighter and she made plans and preparations – more so than she had done for the family at Christmas.

Jim seemed quiet and withdrawn and grew more so as Katharine's pleasure in Elizabeth's visit increased. She feared he guessed the underlying reason for her interest, but still he said nothing.

Elizabeth would bring back medicine into her life – more so than could Anthony for through Elizabeth, Katharine could recapture and conjure up the feel of the hospital. She could not understand herself why, even though she shrank from undertaking any work here in Brackenbeck, as Anthony had suggested, still, against her better judgement, she thirsted for news of her child patients in London. If it had done nothing else, she realised, Brackenbeck had helped sweep away much of the bitterness in her heart that she had fostered in her lonely room in London against her own colleagues in the medical profession – an unreasonable bitterness she realised now.

But Katharine was somewhat thwarted in her intentions, for when Elizabeth had been welcomed to Kendrick House, she soon made it quite clear that she considered herself on holiday.

'Katharine, my dear, I want to forget all about that place for two heavenly weeks,' Elizabeth said in reply to Katharine's questions. Katharine could not prevent the disappointment from showing on her face.

'I think,' Jim said quietly, his eyes never leaving Katharine's face, 'that she has been counting on your visit, Elizabeth, to recapture her life at the hospital.'

'How very perceptive of you,' Katharine said bitterly and saw Elizabeth's eyebrows rise in astonishment. Katharine's remark – totally unlike her – had obviously shocked her friend and indeed, had surprised her husband. But her anger at Elizabeth's refusal to discuss the hospital life with her and finally at Jim having guessed the truth had caused her to vent her chagrin upon her husband.

'I'll have to be going,' he said. 'I'll see you at dinner, Elizabeth.'

And he strode from the room without a backward glance at his wife.

'Kate, dear. I'm sorry if I've disappointed you. But to tell the truth, we've been so short-staffed just lately that I'm so weary with it all. Perhaps,' she added placatingly, 'after a week or so I'll feel more like it, but please,' she raised her hands in mock despair, 'spare me for the moment.'

Katharine sighed.

'I'm sorry,' she said with contrition. 'And I'm even sorrier that Jim saw through me. I didn't want to hurt him.'

'Well, I think you have done,' said the forthright Elizabeth. 'I don't know about you, Kate. A fine man like Jim for a husband and you still hanker after practising as a doctor. And here I am *dying* to meet some handsome young man with a small fortune.'

Katharine smiled, cheered even against her will by Elizabeth's buoyant good humour.

Katharine had invited Anthony to dinner again in the hope that his presence would increase the possibility of the conversation turning to medicine. But because of the incident earlier in the day, at dinner she wished to avoid the topic.

The atmosphere between Katharine and Jim was decidedly strained, though he gave no indication to his guests that anything was wrong. He was courteous and polite towards his wife and helped her as usual whenever necessary. But the tender solicitude was missing. Katharine realised that not only had she hurt Jim because he loved her, but she had also insulted his pride before Elizabeth. And that she knew was unforgivable.

The feeling of tension was somewhat lessened by the fact, which became more obvious as the evening progressed, that Anthony and Elizabeth were immediately mutually attracted. Indeed, so absorbed in each other did they become that had Jim's attitude been at all noticeable to either of them, they would have been far too engrossed in each other to realise it.

The conversation, centred upon general topics, touched lightly here and there, as might be expected, on the subject of medicine, but it certainly did not monopolise the talk. And because, more and more now, Katharine was ashamed of her behaviour, she hated the very sound of the subject and shuddered every time the conversation turned in that direction. She tried to emulate Jim's attitude and play the charming hostess, but as time passed and it was obvious that Anthony and Elizabeth needed little help from anyone else to keep their conversation going, she fell silent. Jim too spoke little, but he seemed to Katharine to be listening intently to what his guests had to say, occasionally adding a comment of his own. And whilst she frequently glanced at him, trying to read his expression, he, on the other hand, never once looked at her directly. His face, usually so easy to read, was a mask of indifference. Only the deep frown between his heavy eyebrows gave any indication of his inner conflict.

'I am longing to see these famous moors of yours,' Elizabeth was saying. Her blue eyes twinkled merrily at Anthony and her dark curls, which she tried to smooth into an elegant style, escaped and curled becomingly round her face. She was wearing a cream-coloured silk chiffon dress covered with tulle and guipure lace, and looked, Katharine thought, utterly charming. Anthony, smiling back at Elizabeth, seemed completely captivated.

'And may I make so bold as to offer to show them to you?'

'Why, I'd be delighted,' she replied in mock surprise, though no one in the room was in much doubt that they both wished to meet again and soon.

And so it was arranged that on the following afternoon Anthony would escort Elizabeth up the hills and on to the moors.

'Of course, I don't expect you will like them,' Anthony said. 'City girls don't you know. Kate doesn't, do you Kate?'

And Anthony and Elizabeth both looked towards her, but not Jim. There was a slight pause as they waited for her answer. And she knew that, though he was not looking at her, Jim too was waiting for her reply.

'In my case, it's rather difficult. I'm one of these stupid people who never value anything until they have lost it. Most likely if I had to leave Brackenbeck now, and the moorland, I should miss it.'

Her remark had deeper meaning than any of the other three could guess. She had left Brackenbeck once and only she would ever know how much she had missed the place, and its people, during her five years away from it. She had lost her ability to be a doctor, and a woman doctor at that. In the process losing her personal fight for the emancipation of women. And she had, at first, bitterly resented the loss. Now, if she were not careful, she could in her own foolishness lose her husband's love. And in so doing, would she, she asked herself, only then find out how much this man really meant to her?

She sighed. It was time she came to terms with life and sorted out her feelings.

The evening ended. And as Jim carried her upstairs later, Katharine put her arms round his neck and buried her face against his shoulder.

'I'm sorry, Jim,' she whispered. 'Please forgive me.'

He laid her gently on the bed and stroked her hair. She saw he was smiling, though his smile was tinged with sadness.

'Forget it, my dear. I try to understand, but sometimes, it is difficult . . .'

Katharine shook her head.

'It's all my fault, Jim. But I do so hate being like this. If only I could walk again, everything would be all right, I know it would.'

'Katharine, please don't . . . oh, never mind,' he sighed distractedly and walked from the room.

Obviously she had said the wrong thing once more. But here she felt that it was Jim who was being unreasonable. Why should he not want her to walk again?

But this was a question she could not answer.

Elizabeth's visit passed all too quickly. And it seemed that Katharine saw little of her, for she spent most of her holiday in Anthony's company, whenever the two could contrive it.

'Oh Kate,' she said on her last morning in Brackenbeck. 'I have been so discourteous to you. Can you forgive me?'

Katharine laughed.

'There is nothing to forgive, Elizabeth. I am only too happy that you have enjoyed your stay. You have, haven't you?'

'Oh Kate, I can't tell you just how much. Kate,' she added in a confidential tone. 'Please don't say anything, not even to Jim, for

I don't know how Anthony feels, but as far as I'm concerned, I've found my handsome young man.'

'But he doesn't have a small fortune,' Katharine smiled at the happy face of her friend.

'Oh *that!* I shan't give that a second thought,' she said, blushing prettily.

'When shall you be seeing him again?'

'I don't know. He hasn't said anything. You see, I may be imagining it all. Perhaps it's nothing more to him than just a casual acquaintanceship.'

'He's taking you to the station this morning, isn't he?'

'Yes.'

'Then I've no doubt he'll make his intentions clear when you have to part. And I want to know, and as Anthony is not likely to tell me, I want a letter from you immediately you get home.'

Elizabeth laughed.

But evidently their expectations were not forthcoming, for when Elizabeth's letters arrived, it told of no 'declaration' from Anthony. In fact, she only casually referred to him in passing. Katharine was disappointed. She had hoped that it was the beginning of a romance, which could culminate in her friend coming to live in Brackenbeck.

The weeks passed and during the summer days, Jim still took Katharine on excursions to the moors. She began to enjoy these outings a little more than she had done previously. And because Jim seemed so much happier here, in the open countryside, she chose their last visit to the moors before winter closed in, on a cool autumn day, to tell him.

'Jim,' she said suddenly as they moved slowly along a rough path, the car jogging up and down. 'Stop the car. I want to tell you something.'

He did so immediately and turned to face her.

'What is it, my dear?' he said as the noisy engine died away.

'Jim, I've something to tell you.'

'Yes?' he prompted gently.

'We – I'm going to have a child,' she heard her voice say in curiously flat tones. She watched his face as the realisation and joy spread over it. He took her hand in his and raised it to his lips.

'My dearest,' his voice was husky.

'You're – you're pleased?'

'Of course, of course. It will be a son. Or a girl like you. Just like you.'

She made no reply.

'You're – you're *not* pleased?' he asked, bewilderment in his tone.

She shrugged and looked away over the flatness of the moor to the rugged outline of the hills, clear-cut against the grey sky.

'I – just don't feel anything.'

He made no reply, but she knew she had hurt him deeply now, and once more she felt ashamed. He had given her his all and she could not even bear his child with joy.

They said little after that and soon Jim turned the motor car towards home.

Their secret remained such for some time. Perhaps because she was seated so much and went out little, none of the usual speculation concerning a young woman married a short time ran amongst the women. Anthony, of course, was told and he attended her. Mary and Tom were taken into their confidence when Katharine reached her fifth month. Mary was overwhelmed and blushed pink with pleasure.

'Oh, how grand it'll be, Katharine. I should like – another, you know,' she confided hesitantly. Katharine still felt that Mary, in her shyness, held her in some awe.

'Perhaps, perhaps, before long ... And then they'd grow up together, wouldn't they? And of course, Kate's not all that much older. Oh, how lovely it will be.'

Katharine nodded and tried to smile, tried to show some interest.

But when the child began to move within her she felt the stirrings of other feelings until now alien to her. It was as if the new life within her was giving Katharine herself new life too. For the first time since she had known of her pregnancy she began to think of the child as a living being with a will and personality of its own.

But over-riding all her other thoughts now grew the fervent desire that by the time her child was born she would be able to walk again. What sort of mother could she hope to be confined to a bathchair, she asked herself?

Katharine had visited the very depths of despair and depression. The only way for her lay upwards and though the way was long and hard at last a glimmer of light lay ahead in the form of her unborn child. Though she began to improve within herself, within her own private thoughts, it was some time before she began, hesitantly, as if feeling her way in the dark, to reach out towards Jim.

And she did not find him wanting. Instinctively he helped her in the way she needed it. Encouraging her interest in their child came naturally, for he could talk of little else.

'It will be a son, or a girl just like you,' he would say not once but a dozen times a week.

'Would you prefer a son, Jim?' Katharine would ask softly.

'Well – yes and no,' he would smile. 'I should love a daughter just as much and yet . . .'

'The old, old, feeling,' Katharine would smile too, though a little sadly, 'male superiority.'

'No, no, Katharine, it's not . . .'

'But it is.'

'Every man wants a son to carry on the family name.'

'But why shouldn't a girl carry on the name? Why is a girl so inferior?'

'They're not inferior, just . . .'

'Just what?'

'Well, they are the weaker sex.'

'Only because tradition says so.'

Jim sighed. Katharine saw the frown form once more on his forehead and knew it was time to change the subject.

But the frown returned again the day she first mentioned the desire to try and walk again, outlining to Jim her plan for exercising her legs to try and strengthen them.

'You'll try no such thing, Katharine,' he said severely. 'You'll hurt yourself.'

'Of course I shan't. If I'm very careful and take it slowly.'

'I forbid you to try it,' he said pacing up and down the drawing-room whilst her eyes followed him.

She looked at him appealingly.

'Jim, please I . . .'

'If you won't think of yourself, Katharine, please think of our child. Think what harm you could do if you were to fall, apart from further injury you may do to yourself.'

He paused and swung round to face her, his eyes blazing and hostile. Katharine had seen his many and varied moods, but never had she seen him so heatedly angry.

'You're a doctor. How can you be so foolish?'

She realised he was right. However careful she was, she might easily fall and injure herself and her baby especially now she had the extra weight to carry, she acknowledged.

'All right, all right. You win,' she said bitterly and covered her face with her hands.

He came and knelt beside her chair, his anger dying swiftly.

'Katharine, my love, I don't mean to be cruel and hard, but can't you see how much you mean to me? I couldn't bear you to hurt yourself further.'

'But I *must* walk again, I *must*,' her voice was muffled, but she knew he heard her.

When she raised her head, he had left the room swiftly and silently.

She never mentioned the subject again to Jim and though for a few days there was constraint between them, gradually the frown softened and left his forehead and she thought he had forgotten the incident.

Anthony came regularly to see her, as a doctor and also as a friend and he dined with them frequently.

'I see you're beginning to look a little more like the old Kate,' he said one morning on one of his official visits, when Jim was out visiting Tom at the quarry.

She smiled, warmly and genuinely.

'And have you thought any more about my suggestion as regards giving talks to the women of the village?' he said.

'Oh Anthony,' Katharine said, her face falling. 'I really couldn't.'

He shrugged and shook his head.

'I wish you would, I really do. There's so much in the way of hygiene you could teach them. And I think it would be one of those cases where they'd take it better from a woman than from a man. These country folk are so goodhearted. You'll go a long way before you find kinder folk, but they just don't understand that unhygienic living can cause all sorts of trouble, a regular breeding ground for disease . . .'

'Please, Anthony, please,' her voice became high-pitched.

'All right, all right. But you're wasting your time and talents. You're a trained doctor, remember?'

She could not fail to notice the sarcasm apparent in his tone.

'I can't,' she whispered, and refused to meet his eyes, afraid of the reproach she would read in them.

'Forget it then,' he said lightly and with his natural good humour restored he changed the subject abruptly.

But after he had gone, Katharine was left alone with her thoughts before Jim returned, painful and guilty thoughts she found them to be. She couldn't do it now, really she couldn't, not with the child coming. But later perhaps, if she got to walk again, then things might be different – she could take up medicine again . . .

Chapter Eight

Christmas that year was a quiet family affair. The end of the nine months approached and the date Anthony predicted for Katharine's confinement came – and passed.

'What can be wrong?' Jim asked anxiously for the hundredth time it seemed to Katharine.

'Nothing. He's just lazy,' she answered patiently.

'You haven't been – well – trying to walk or anything, Katharine, have you?'

She looked up into his dark, worried eyes and was thankful that she could answer him truthfully.

'No, Jim, I promise you I haven't.'

He sighed with relief.

'I realised you were right – at least until after the baby is born,' she added.

'Now, Katharine . . .'

'Let's change the subject,' she said brightly, but she knew she could not deceive Jim for long.

The days passed by slowly whilst they waited and Jim grew more and more impatient and anxious. And so it was with profound relief that Katharine was able to say to him one evening in the New Year.

'Jim, I think my time has come. Would you carry me up to the bedroom and then fetch Anthony.'

He sprang out of his chair.

'Oh Katharine, Katharine. How can you be so calm? Are you all right? Is the pain bad?'

She laughed.

''Tis a wonderful feeling. I feel alive for the first time in years.'

She reached up and as he bent down towards her she put her arms round his neck and kissed him with gentle fervour. He responded and in his kiss she felt his concern, his love, his excited expectation in the birth of their child.

As another sharp pain leapt through her, he lifted her gently and carried her up the wide stairs to the room which had been specially prepared weeks ago for this event. Even though she was so much heavier, Jim carried her like a feather, such was this man's strength.

He laid her gently on the bed, kissed her forehead and left the room swiftly.

'Mrs. Johnson, Mrs. Johnson,' she heard him calling as he ran downstairs.

She heard the woman's footsteps come from the servants' quarters, a muted exchange of conversation, the slam of the front door as Jim hurried to fetch Anthony, and, as Mrs. Johnson came into the room, the distant sound of Jim's motor car engine bursting into life.

'Now, my dear,' said the older woman, her pleasant face wreathed in smiles. 'This is what we've all been waiting for. We'll soon have the little fellow here.'

Despite the pains which were becoming more rapid, Katharine smiled at Mrs. Johnson's faith that the arrival would be a son and heir.

Girls, thought Katharine ruefully, were still second-best.

'Well, Kate,' Anthony boomed as he strode into the room, 'at last you're going to do something useful, eh?'

Katharine saw Mrs. Johnson's startled glance and realised she misunderstood Anthony's manner. This was not callousness on his part, Katharine knew. It was merely his brusque way of letting her know how foolish she had been and at the same time how pleased he was that the black days were almost over. She grinned at him over the bed covers, her old, cheerful self reasserting itself more quickly than anyone could have imagined. Here, out of her bathchair, she felt the same as any other woman giving birth to her first-born.

It was a difficult birth from Katharine's point of view though her son suffered no ill affects whatsoever and bawled lustily and immediately on arrival.

But Katharine suffered far more pain than she had imagined she would. She could not, brave though she was, resist moaning softly to herself. Anthony, however, seemed to accept the pain cheerfully.

'You're cruel, Anthony Stafford, absolutely heartless,' she bantered him afterwards when it was all over and the pain had subsided a little.

He sat on the bed and grinned at her.

'I can't help being a little pleased because you're suffering pain.'

'What!' Katharine almost shrieked at him, though half in jest.

'Don't you realise, Dr. Kendrick, that it could be an excellent sign that you could regain all feeling, could recover – perhaps completely.'

Katharine's eyes shone.

'Anthony,' she whispered. 'Do you really think I shall be able to walk again?'

'Now, now, don't get too excited. I don't want to raise false hopes, but you know everyone has always been baffled as to the exact nature of your paralysis, but I see no reason why you shouldn't recover completely.'

Further conversation was suspended as Mrs. Johnson brought Katharine's baby to her.

''Tis time that husband of yours saw his son,' Anthony said rising. 'And now you're safely delivered of your child, I'm off to London for a few days to see Elizabeth.'

'Oh, Anthony, I'm so glad – I didn't know you had kept in touch.'

'Yes – regularly,' he grinned down at her.

He paused in the doorway and looked back at her.

'Well, Kate my dear,' he said softly. 'By the look on your face, I would think you'd found your vocation right there.' And he nodded in the direction of the child in her arms, then he closed the door before she had time to reply.

Katharine looked down at the small wrinkled face. He was sleeping now. Her eyes wandered over the tiny features. So small yet so perfect.

Her son. This was her son.

When she looked up again, Jim was standing at the foot of the bed watching her.

'Jim,' she whispered, and found her voice not quite steady. 'Jim, here is your son.'

He nodded, not speaking, and when he moved closer to bend over her and the sleeping child, she understood why. Unshed tears of joy filled his eyes.

'Hold him, Jim.'

'No, I couldn't. I might hurt him.'

She laughed.

'Of course you won't. He'll not break.'

Gently Jim took the child and the pride and love apparent in his face was, to Katharine, worth all the pain she had suffered.

'Jim,' she said, suddenly remembering. 'Anthony thinks that there may be a chance that my back will improve. I may be able to walk again.'

Jim looked up, the bemused pleasure in his face dying a little. A wary look came into his eyes. He seemed about to speak, but then decided against it and turned his attention back to the small white bundle in his strong arms. But the unspoiled joy was gone from his face. Some cloud had crossed the day and Katharine could not understand why.

She made no further reference to the hopes which she now nurtured that one day she may be able to walk again. For the present she was willing to glory in her child and in Jim's obvious happiness. Gradually, he too seemed to forget her remark for it was surely that which had caused him to look downcast.

'What are we to call him?' Jim asked. 'We still haven't decided and the little fellow must have a name.'

'I should rather like to call him after my father. But would you mind?'

'Do you know,' Jim said soberly. 'It seems rather dreadful, but you haven't told me anything about your family. I don't even know your father's name.'

Katharine felt ashamed.

'I know, it's my fault. His name was Jonathan.'

'Why, that's a grand name. Jonathan Kendrick.'

'He was a doctor.'

His eyes searched her face.

'Hoping he'll take after his grandfather?'

'No, not particularly,' she said truthfully. 'It hasn't done me a great deal of good, nor, come to that, my father.'

'Why not – for your father, I mean?'

'We lived in a very poor district of London, but my father never refused a patient and more often than not his services were never paid for.'

Jim nodded.

'I can understand that. But Katharine, why did you become a doctor then, if you knew it meant such hardship in certain cases?'

She lay back against the pillows and her mind flew back over the years and she was a small girl standing beside her father. She could hear his words.

'You shall become a doctor, one of the first women doctors, Katharine my child, you shall pave the way for other women.'

And all she had wanted was to see his pride in her justified. Besides which, she had lived and breathed medicine since childhood.

'He lived just long enough to see me enter university,' she told Jim. 'He was so pleased, so proud. I think he wanted a son to carry on after him. But mother could have no more children, so I had to take the place of a son.'

'But did you really want to become a doctor, from your own point of view, or was it solely because your father wanted you to do so?'

'Oh I wanted to, I loved it, and I also knew, or thought I knew, that I should always have to earn my own living.'

'How do you mean?'

She grinned sheepishly.

'I couldn't imagine anyone ever wanting to marry me.'

'My dearest Katharine, how wrong you were.' And he kissed her hand.

'Jonathan shall do whatever he pleases, so long as he's happy,' Katharine said.

'Agreed. But give him a few years yet?'

And they laughed at their own parental pride. At that moment a curious ringing sound reached them faintly, as if coming from a long distance.

'Ah, they're ringing t'gavelock,' Jim said, his Yorkshire accent more pronounced as Katharine had noticed before when he felt something deeply.

'The what?' she asked.

'It's at the quarry. I didn't think we'd hear them from here, but the wind must be in this direction, carrying the sound.'

'But what is it, Jim?'

'The quarrymen suspend a long, iron crowbar on chains and then about six or seven of them stand beside it and strike it with their iron hammers. Listen.'

Jim crossed to the window and opened it. She could hear now the rhythmic ringing from the quarry – still distant – but there was no mistaking it, now Jim had explained it to her.

'Why are they doing it? Why have I not heard it before?'

'The gavelock's rung in celebration of important events in the lives of the villagers. This particular occasion is in honour of this little fellow.'

And Jim bent over the cradle once more as if he could not see enough of his son, nor cease to wonder at the perfection of the child.

And so Jonathan Kendrick took his place in the Kendrick family and indeed at Kendrick House he soon became the most important personage in the household. Katharine's life revolved round her small son, and whilst she tried not to indulge him, she at last had something worthwhile to occupy her mind and time – at least, when she was allowed to play with him by the stern, but devoted nanny. The appointment of a nanny had caused a quarrel between Jim and his wife. Katharine clung to her child as being her means of recovering from her depression, but at last she had had to admit that Jim was right in his views, that she could not look after her infant son perfectly from a bathchair.

'Other women do – what about those who cannot afford to employ a nanny?' she had asked.

Jim had sighed.

'I know – I know. But we can, so there's no need to run the risk of you hurting yourself or Jonathan.'

'If only . . .' Katharine had been about to say if only she could walk, but had stopped short. On so many occasions it had distressed her husband that she would not invite his further anger on this occasion.

But during the time she spent with her son, she recaptured much of her old spirit. At last, she thought, she was cured of melancholia. At last she could begin to look forward in life and plan for the future. A worthwhile future.

About eight months after the birth of her child, in the middle of August, when the village was bathed day after day in sunshine and it became so hot, almost unbearably hot that children ran about near-naked, Anthony called at Kendrick House one evening.

He came into the drawing-room and having greeted Jim and Katharine, sank wearily into a chair. Katharine saw that he looked desperately tired, his eyes dark-ringed, his fair hair dishevelled.

'Whatever's wrong?' Jim asked.

Anthony's eyes met Katharine's and she was shocked to see there was no trace of the smile she was so used to seeing on his gay face. Lines of worry and weariness etched age into his young face, as if he carried the troubles of the world on his broad shoulders and yet was unable to bear the burden.

And there was something else in his eyes, Katharine knew, even before he spoke. Reproach. She read reproach in his eyes as he looked at her.

He dropped his head into his hands and his voice was muffled as he spoke.

'Jake Ford's lad's ill. Very ill.'

'What is it?' Katharine asked sharply.

'I can't be absolutely sure as yet. But all the symptoms could point to – typhoid.'

'Oh my God,' exclaimed Jim.

And Katharine's heart went cold.

Anthony raised his head slowly.

'The weather's been so abominably hot. Food's gone bad, as they eat it almost, and Mrs. Ford's not as careful as she might be where cleanliness is concerned. Then again, mothers allow their children to play in the beck, not, mark you, up near the source, where the water is clean and pure, but below the village after all the housewives have thrown their dirty water and waste into it. I've no proof, of course, as to exactly how he has contracted it. There could be several explanations, and, unfortunately, several causes.'

And his eyes met Katharine's once more. The silence hung in the room between them.

'You're blaming me,' Katharine said softly, at last.

Before Anthony could answer Jim broke in.

'Whatever do you mean? What can you possibly have to do with it?'

'Anthony asked me to give talks to the women of the village about hygiene and general health problems – you know,' she paused and looked down at her hands lying on her lap. 'And I refused.'

'I knew nothing of this,' Jim said.

Katharine looked up from Anthony to Jim.

'But Anthony said he'd discussed it with you and you had no objections.'

'I never said anything of the sort.'

They both looked towards Anthony.

'I spoke to you about it one day about her joining in the village activities, don't you remember?'

'But I thought you meant socially, not to practise medicine. I should never have agreed.'

'I'm sorry, I'm sorry,' Anthony waved his hand distractedly.

'Forget it now, anyway,' said Jim. 'You've more important things to talk about.'

'But it wouldn't have been practising medicine,' persisted Anthony. 'Just a small way in which she could have been some use.'

'Since you insist on discussing it, she's plenty of use here,' bellowed Jim, his face dark and angry.

'Please, please,' Katharine begged. 'Don't have an unnecessary argument *now*.'

'No, you're right Katharine. We must think what we can do,' Jim said, his quick temper calming rapidly.

'How many are there in the family, who may be in danger of contracting it?' Katharine asked.

'There's Jake and his wife, of course, three children besides William, who has it, a baby of six months or so and – Louise Banroyd.'

'Louise? Is she still with the Fords?' Katharine asked.

The two men exchanged a look.

'After you left Brackenbeck we decided the best thing to do would be to let Louise stay with the Fords,' Jim said.

'But how can Mrs. Ford keep her? They're poor enough without another mouth to feed.'

Jim moved restlessly about the room.

'I give her some money for the child,' he muttered.

'Ay, and more than enough for one. He just about keeps the whole family,' put in Anthony.

'Then why should they appear so poor?' she asked.

'Drink,' said Anthony briefly, and Jim paced the floor.

'Who, Jake?'

'Mostly, though I believe Annie Ford's not averse to it.'

'Wouldn't Louise have been better with someone else?'

'Yes, we did try. But the child threw a fit every time we took her somewhere else. After all, Grannie Banroyd was just as poor, the child was brought up to it.'

'You should have taken her away, she would have settled down in time. Children have short memories,' Katharine said.

'Can you isolate the family, or is the whole valley in danger?' Jim asked Anthony.

The young doctor sighed.

'I really don't know. I can, of course, give strict instructions for them to remain in their house, but whether they'll obey is another matter. Of course, when word gets round, the other villagers will keep their distance, no doubt.'

'But are you quite sure it is typhoid?' Katharine asked.

'No, I told you, I can't be absolutely sure yet, not for another day or so, but I must take the precautions just in case . . .'

'If I had done as you asked Anthony,' Katharine said slowly, 'do you think this could have been avoided?'

There was a pause. The silence hung heavy in the room between the three of them. Katharine looked at Anthony's face, usually so good-humoured, now solemn and lined with worry.

'Who can say. Maybe, maybe not,' was his non-committal reply.

Even Jim remained silent and she felt that, despite his earlier words, he now realised that she could have done something useful amongst his people and had she done so, perhaps this tragedy could have been avoided.

'I must go,' Anthony said heavily and rose slowly as if he feared to face the task awaiting him. Jim accompanied him to the front door and when he came back his face wore the worried frown Katharine knew so well.

'I wish he had not come here, Katharine,' he said. 'Just because he is a doctor he is not immune to infection, and after all, besides ourselves, we have Jonathan to consider.'

'Oh no, no,' Katharine cried as realisation hit her. 'If he were to catch it . . .'

'We shall have to take care, great care. We must not come into contact with him. Nanny must be isolated in the nursery with him. But meanwhile, I must find out what I can do for the Ford family.'

'Don't go to the house, don't go anywhere near them, or you'll bring Jonathan into worse danger,' she felt the panic rise within her.

Jim's dark gaze was on her face.

'What is this, Katharine? From you, a doctor – putting your own family first before the patient?'

His sarcasm was not lost on her. She buried her head in her

hands, her emotions so confused she did not know herself what she felt. When she looked up again, Jim had left the room.

In the quietness of the room whilst Jim was out, Katharine had time for thought. She began to question herself in a way which she had never done before.

Vividly the pictures of her life and various attitudes towards life came before her. Life as a girl in her father's surgery: fascinated by the bottles and potions he mixed, drawn by tender solicitude for the feelings of others to want to heal people and eliminate suffering as her father did so ably and so nobly. Again she could hear her father's voice bemoaning the fact that he had no son to follow him. Was it then that the seeds of medicine were sown in her mind? Was it merely an overwhelming desire to please her father, as Jim had once suggested? Or had she really wanted to become a doctor in her own right?

Her years at medical school: the fight for equality, or as near equal rights as she was ever likely to get, became a challenge in itself, quite apart from the task of qualifying. She could see now that independence had become second nature to her, feeling, as she had at that time, that she would never marry, that she must make a career for herself, and find the fulfilment in that career which most women seek in family life.

And then her coming to Brackenbeck: her meeting with the powerful personality of Jim Kendrick and her decision to leave him in favour of medicine. Had it been the right decision? It could never be proved. And whilst no one would say that she had not done useful work before she became paralysed, she had not made a great name for herself, nor even done much to make things easier in the future for her own sex, in the battle for the emancipation of women.

Instead, here she was married to Jim Kendrick, with a small son, confined to a bathchair. Never, in her wildest moment had she anticipated such a life for herself.

And now it appeared she had failed in her allegiance to the medical profession. She had taken years to train, time and money. And when she was needed, here in Brackenbeck, even if only in a small way, but still needed, she had turned away, her bitterness and withdrawal from life clouding her mind and blinding her reason. Katharine felt more ashamed than ever of her behaviour over the past few months and, indeed, years. And in her shame, the picture of Jim's face came into her mind. What a one-sided affair their marriage had been. How much love and care he had lavished upon her only to be met with disinterest and a cold heart on her part.

Katharine gave a sob and the tears, which she had held so long, in check, flowed freely. And it was as if her tears washed away all the bitterness and misunderstanding from her heart and when her weeping ceased, she found she could for the first time since she had become confined to her chair, face the situation with calmness and detachment.

Jim's last bitter remark before he left the room haunted her. She had failed not only in medicine, but as a wife and mother too. But her common sense, which had deserted her for so long, now began to re-assert itself.

The old Katharine was coming back to life. And the old Katharine was not one to admit defeat. There was still time to make amends even though her past behaviour would leave its mark on Jim as it would upon herself.

And slowly, too, the realisation came to her that she returned Jim's love in full measure now. It was not a sudden, overwhelming revelation, but a gradual recognition that through his care and tenderness he had won her love in return. But still she could not tell him, could not put her feelings into words.

The news of the Ford household drove all other considerations from the minds of Jim and Katharine. He, preoccupied for most of the time with easing the burden of the Fords, was away from home a great deal. Katharine, left alone, worried incessantly about the fear of an epidemic and always there was the nagging thought that she could have prevented it.

'What news?' she asked Jim each time he returned in the evening. And on the third evening after Anthony's visit, Jim sat down heavily in his armchair and leant back, his face lined with tiredness.

'Louise has caught it.'

'Oh no,' whispered Katharine.

'No one else – at the moment,' he added, though his words were but small consolation.

Anthony did not come to Kendrick House again, but Katharine knew that he and Jim met each day in the valley. It was as if a shadow hung over Brackenbeck, whilst each family waited in fear to see if their children contracted the disease. But for the moment the illness remained confined to the Ford household.

'Anthony's puzzled,' said Jim one evening, when he returned home. 'He feels that if it is typhoid, then other children would be bound to get it. Will Ford's a gregarious young ruffian.'

'There's hardly been time for anyone else to have contracted it from contact with William, but one would think other children would have contracted it from the same source,' Katharine mused. 'I suppose it *is* typhoid?'

'That's what Anthony's beginning to wonder now. But the children have all the symptoms he says – you know, headache, fever, vomiting and the rest.'

'Mmm,' Katharine said thoughtfully. 'I wish I could see them for myself.'

'You'll do no such thing,' Jim replied sharply, the angry frown deepening on his forehead. 'If you can't think of yourself, for heaven's sake think of Jonathan.'

Katharine smiled.

'I wasn't serious. You know I wouldn't do anything to endanger Jonathan.'

Although he did not reply, Jim looked none too sure about that. He sighed and ran his hand through his dark hair.

'I can think of nothing more I can do to help them. Can you?'

'No, I can't I'm afraid. Anthony will be doing everything medically.'

Distantly they heard the front doorbell.

'I wonder who it can be,' Jim murmured.

A few moments elapsed before Mrs. Johnson showed Anthony into the room. He held up his hand as he saw Jim about to speak.

'I know what you're thinking – that I'm bringing infection here perhaps. But I have news that I think you want to know.'

'Good news,' asked Katharine anxiously, 'or bad?'

'Both,' replied Anthony. 'Firstly, the good news – it's not typhoid.'

'Thank God,' breathed Jim.

Katharine passed her hand over her forehead in a gesture of thankfulness but said nothing.

'It's severe food poisoning.'

'Well, there's no wonder you thought it was typhoid – or could be,' exclaimed Katharine. 'The first symptoms of both food poisoning of certain types and typhoid are often similar.'

'Exactly,' said Anthony slapping his thigh.

'That certainly is good news,' said Jim. 'Even though the children are obviously suffering, at least there's no danger.'

Anthony's face sobered swiftly.

'Ah, now that, I'm afraid, is where you're wrong.'

'What?' Katharine and Jim spoke simultaneously.

'Louise is very sick indeed. I fear she may not recover. She's such an undernourished little soul that she's no stamina to fight the infection.' He shook his head sadly. 'You should see her – such a pathetic sight. Poor child.'

'Anthony, you must try not to get involved,' Katharine said softly.

'There are times when even a hard-hearted doctor becomes involved. This is one of those times for me, Kate. I feel helplessly inadequate.'

She sighed.

'Yes, I know.' She remembered vividly her own feelings as she had watched Grannie Banroyd slip away from life. And now Grannie Banroyd's grand-daughter was dying too. It was ironic, Katharine thought bitterly, that she had failed to save the old lady and had been blamed by the villagers and now, perhaps because she had refused to give instruction to those same villagers, Louise had been given some infected food and her life was in danger.

It seemed her failures were synonymous with the Banroyd family.

'Is she really as bad as that?' she asked, willing Anthony to reply negatively. But he was unable to do so.

'I'm afraid so, yes.'

'What about hospital?'

'It would do no good, Kate.'

'You're to spare no expense, Anthony,' Jim put in. 'You know that, don't you?'

'Yes, of course.'

Anthony left some little time later, and behind him he left a shadow over Kendrick House. Katharine blamed herself for her own part, or rather lack of it, in this. And Jim seemed strangely silent.

Perhaps, she thought, now that he knew it really has something to do with unhygienic ways, he does blame me, knowing that I could have done something to improve conditions.

The following days were agony for Katharine. Whilst her small son giggled and laughed in his cradle, restored once more to the family circle now that the identity of the illness was known, she was unable to respond to his cherubic appeal.

Her mind and heart were in the small cottage in the valley with Louise, though physically she remained confined to her invalid chair at Kendrick House. She and Jim did not go out on their usual drives, nor indeed did he spend as much time with her.

At first she had thought it was because he was involved in doing what he could to help the Fords, but gradually she realised that this could not be taking up so much of his time, for there was little he could actually do but wait for news from Anthony. She hesitated to ask him outright how he was spending his time, but she became more aware of his change of attitude towards her. Perhaps, she told herself, it was preoccupation, which could naturally be attributed to anxiety for Louise, as indeed was Katharine so concerned.

Four days after Anthony had told them of Louise's serious illness, Jim returned home during the morning.

Katharine knew immediately he entered the room that he had grave news.

'Is it Louise?' she asked softly.

He nodded and said quietly,

'She died this morning.'

There was a silence in the room. Jim went to stand before the window looking out over the valley.

'You blame me?' Katharine said, her voice strangely shrill unlike her normal low tones.

'No – no, of course not,' Jim replied irritably, still not looking at her. But there had been a visible change in his attitude towards her since the children's illness, which was even more pronounced now that the illness had proved fatal.

She said no more but she did not believe his denial.

Kendrick House was subdued over the next few days and weeks. Only Jonathan, burbling happily or bawling lustily in his cradle, remained unperturbed by the events. The village once again turned out in their dozens to attend Louise's funeral. Only Katharine was a noticeable absentee.

It was a hot day, still and silent. The quarry machinery was stilled, even the farmers left their fields. Katharine, high on the hillside in the garden of Kendrick House, watched the distant procession winding through the valley towards the church. They looked to her like a colony of ants, but the measured pace of the mournful procession was far removed from the scurrying creatures to which she likened it.

Again, as at Grannie Banroyd's funeral, she was an outsider. And again, she felt herself blamed.

Anthony had asked her to help him and she had failed to respond to his request and the villagers' need.

'I will not fail again,' she murmured to herself as the procession reached the church. And there, sitting in the bright sunlight, alone on the hillside overlooking Brackenbeck, Katharine found herself again. Her melancholy of the past few years was over. Replaced by the natural grief and remorse for Louise's death, she had rid herself of the destructive self-pity and introspection which had clouded her reason and dulled her natural spirit for so long. There remained only her original personality. And with the return of her natural tenacity came the overwhelming desire to walk again, stronger than ever before: to lead a full life once more. Not, she knew now, to carve a career for herself in medicine, for her life was now bound up with her husband and son, both of whom filled her heart with love.

But perhaps, still, there was work for her in the valley. Anthony would not find her wanting the next time he asked for her help.

She was anxious to tell Jim of the change which had taken place, of her new-found strength, of her realisation of the truth, but his attitude towards her had changed and she found communication with him impossible.

Outwardly, there were few signs and an outsider would have seen no indication, but Katharine knew that although he was as attentive as ever for her welfare, there was a change. For a time she was cast down with despair again and her previous misery threatened to engulf her once more. She had left matters too late. Her own stupidity had lost her his love. But she had recovered sufficiently and found enough strength of purpose to realise that perhaps she could by her own efforts, recapture Jim's love.

And Katharine became firmly convinced that the only way she could do this was to walk again. She was sure that he was now tired of a crippled wife, that he regretted his sacrifice in marrying an invalid. In secret she began to exercise her useless limbs. With her medical knowledge she knew what was likely to be of the greatest aid to recovery, though she too could not understand the cause of her paralysis any more than her doctors. She exercised to strengthen the lifeless muscles, each day progressing a little farther. It took time and although she was impatient for results her common sense, coupled with her knowledge, told her that she must be patient.

She told Jim nothing of this and whilst each day he left Kendrick House on his own business, often now taking little Kate, Mary's child, with him again, and even occasionally his small son in a wicker cradle perched on the seat of his motor at his side, not once did he take his wife out.

Alone Katharine persevered. She did not wish even Anthony to know, nor indeed anyone. This she must do alone.

The days passed into autumn and the bleak Yorkshire winter

was upon them again. The children's outings with Jim grew fewer, but still he was out in all weathers and most of the time Katharine knew not where.

Had he been a lesser man, she might have had doubts as to his faithfulness, but it never crossed her mind that Jim Kendrick, a man of his strength of character would even contemplate such a thing. And she was right. If things were not all they could be between man and wife, he was not a man to find cheap consolation. Besides, there was his son, in whom his pride was unlimited. Jim Kendrick would do nothing to bring disgrace upon his small son.

Jonathan grew and was a happy child. Katharine would marvel that such a sunny-natured child could have been borne by such a miserable creature as she had been at that time. His smiling round face was the delight of both his parents and in moments of mutual admiration for their son, it seemed that everything was right between them.

It was on one of these occasions that Katharine hesitantly approached the subject of her complete recovery.

'Jim, I really think I shall be able to walk again. I feel so much stronger and I've been exercising regularly. Will you help me to try and walk a little. I need your support. But I'm sure I . . .'

The dark frown appeared immediately on his forehead and anger flashed in his eyes.

'You will attempt nothing of the sort, Katharine, I've told you before. I forbid you to do so.'

'But Jim . . .'

He paced the floor whilst his small son's puzzled eyes followed his father's movements. His little face was unusually sober.

'No buts, I mean it,' he said, his deep voice ringing through the room.

A whimper escaped Jonathan.

'Jim, you're frightening the child.'

'I'm sorry, but you started this. You know how it worries me. You'll do yourself untold harm and end up worse than ever.'

'I could not be much worse,' Katharine replied, her anger aroused too now. A pitiful wail arose from Jonathan. Katharine leant forward from her chair and picked him from his cradle.

'Jim, please let's discuss it calmly, there's no need to frighten Jonathan.'

'No, no, I'm sorry,' he said swiftly and took the child from her. He carried the boy around the room talking softly to him and soon the sunny smiles appeared once more on the child's face.

'You're being so unreasonable, Jim. I know what is wise to do and it will take a long time, but I'm sure I can learn to walk again.'

He sat down opposite her and held the child to him. She was amazed at the bleak, hopeless look in his eyes.

'Then I suppose,' he said slowly and sadly, 'if you have made up your mind to it, I cannot stop you.'

'You can't really *want* to prevent me, if there is a chance that I can walk again, Jim?' she asked incredulously.

But her husband did not answer and avoided her eyes.

The weeks and months passed and the chasm between them grew deeper. Whilst Katharine fought alone to walk again, Jim drew further away from her. He seemed to devote himself entirely to his son. The boy became his life and Katharine began to feel excluded from their close relationship. Once more she felt an outsider from her husband and now even from her own child, the being to whom she had given life.

But a child as young as Jonathan does not divide its love into unequal parts for its parents. Jonathan continued to respond to his mother as he had always done and at these times she would see the pain in Jim's eyes.

Could he be jealous of his own son's love for his mother?

Whatever was wrong with Jim? He was a changed personality. Or something so great was disturbing him as to cloud his reason, she thought. But she could not bring herself to question him. Perhaps the time would come, but it was not now.

The day came when she took a first step. She felt the thrill run through her as she realised her hope was now a reality. She pushed her right foot forward and found it responded. And although she was shaky and her step like that of a drunken man, she was walking.

She sank back to her bathchair and willed herself to calmness. But the excitement and pleasure were almost unbearable.

And there was no one there to share this moment with her. How she wished Jim was at her side. She could hardly wait to tell him. But no, she thought, I will not tell him until I can walk properly.

And so she kept her secret for a few days more. The difficult part was now over. Each day she gained in strength and her complete recovery was swift now that she had overcome the barrier of the first step alone.

When she could walk right round the drawing-room quite naturally, she decided it was time to tell her husband.

Katharine was half afraid and half delighted with her news. Afraid for Jim's reaction and delighted that at last she could look forward again to a full life. A life with her son, and if he wished it, at her husband's side.

No more sitting at home in a bathchair whilst Jim jaunted out. No more watching her son from a distance whilst he played. No more a watcher, from now on she was a participant in everything.

When Jonathan was abed and the servants in their own quarters after dinner, Katharine decided, was the time to tell him.

'Anthony's coming to dinner tonight,' Jim announced when he arrived home.

'Oh no,' Katharine said, before she could stop herself. She had wanted this evening to themselves.

This evening was to be so special.

'You've never minded before.' A dark cloud crossed his eyes. 'I'm sorry if I should have given you more warning but our table is always well-stocked. I see no need for more preparation.'

'It's not that, it's . . .' she faltered.

'Well?' he asked sharply.

'It's nothing, Jim. It will keep.'

She saw the question in his eyes but did not enlighten him. She wanted the moment of telling him to be unspoilt – perfect.

And so she spent the evening in a turmoil of anticipation. She heard little of the conversation which passed between Jim and Anthony until Anthony spoke directly to her.

'You seem preoccupied this evening, Kate,' he smiled. 'Anything worrying you?'

'No – no. What could there be?' And she glanced at Jim. He was not looking at her, but gazing out of the long window down across the darkened valley.

But she knew Anthony had seen her quick glance at her husband and realised that he would understand things were not entirely smooth between Jim and his wife. She sighed to herself. Now that the time had come to tell Jim, she wished she could get it over. But Anthony's visit had prolonged the agony of waiting. The evening dragged on. She knew she was being a poor hostess, but could not help herself. Over and over in her mind, she rehearsed the words she would use to tell Jim.

At last Anthony left and when Jim returned to the drawing-room, she saw that he was not in the best of moods to receive her news and she was tempted to put off the moment.

But the last few hours had shown her that waiting was almost worse.

'Jim, I have something to tell you.'

'Well?' His tone was discouraging.

'Watch.'

Slowly and carefully she heaved herself up from her chair. She stood facing him and slowly walked towards him.

She was unprepared for the misery in his eyes, the lost, hopeless look. She lost her concentration on walking, to which she still needed to give effort and thought.

'Jim!' She held out her hands as she began to fall. He caught and supported her, but did not hold her to him.

She looked up into his face and tried to read his expression.

'Jim,' she said softly, pleadingly. 'What is it? Whatever is the matter? Why don't you want me to walk again?'

'Oh Katharine, my love!' he murmured, burying his head in her neck, his voice hoarse with emotion. His arms were round her now, with the strength of desperation.

After a moment he raised his head again.

Again the closed expression came into his eyes. He was master of his emotions once more.

'I'm sorry.'

He held her at arms length.

'I should not have embarrassed you.' He saw that she was able to stand on her own and turned away from her.

Katharine watched him in silence, her heart heavy with disappointment and fear. She had thought that everything would come miraculously right when she walked again, but it had only served to make matters worse.

'When will you be leaving?' he asked.

'Leaving? What *are* you talking about?'

He swung round.

'Well, you've nothing to stay here for now, have you? Now you can walk, you'll be wanting to get back to that hospital in London.'

'So *that's* it!'

'What is?' he said, immediately on the defensive.

'Why you didn't want me to walk again. You thought if I walked again, I would walk away from Brackenbeck – back to medicine.'

'Well, won't you?' he said bitterly.

And the unspoken words lay between them – you did once before.

'No, not this time,' she said softly. 'I've found my true love. I'm here to stay.'

'You mean – you mean . . .' he said.

'I mean I love you, Jim. And I'm here for keeps, if you'll have me?'

'*Have* you!' And he covered the distance between them in huge strides. 'Katharine, I was so afraid.'

'Oh, Jim, Jim. Have you so little faith in my love for you?'

'But,' he shook his head. 'You've never said it before. Not until now.'

Her arms tightened round his neck.

'Well, I have now,' she said mischievously. 'Fancy you thinking I would leave you and little Jonathan. What a dreadful picture you have of me.'

'Katharine, please – I –' he said with contrition.

'I'm only teasing, Jim my dearest,' she laughed.

Jim smiled then grinned. And then he too laughed aloud.

And their laughter rang through Kendrick House and echoed through the valley of Brackenbeck.